VALENDRIAL, INTO THE FADE

DaviJones

DaviJones

ISBN-13: 979-8-218-38945-1

Cover design by: Perchance.org/ Davijones
Library of Congress Control Number: 2018675309
Printed in the United States of America

Dedication:
The quality of being dedicated or committed to a task or
purpose.

This book is dedicated to you, dear, dear reader, for every fantasy
you ever had and those to come. Safe journey, my friends. May
there always be a good book in hand and a story to experience.
Thank you so much for experiencing this one with me. (Your
patience with my grammar is always appreciated.) Also, my
family and friends, your encouragement, love, constant patience,
and support are everything.
Thank you.

CONTENTS

PROLOGUE

There is a lull of an altered state of mind, registered, just before I'm grabbed from behind in a darkened room.

"Visiting me in the darkness now? Isn't that nice?"

A rough voice sounds in my ear. A gasp escapes my lips as the stranger's arms grab my own in the darkness. Their other arm encircles my waist as their lips press against mine. I taste warm cognac, making his breath sweet. His fingers gripping my arm release me to run his palm up to my shoulder, pulling me closer and gripping the base of my hair, pins containing my updo cascading down in silky black sheets around my shoulders.

His height intimidates and excites me, his shoulders hunching and drawing into me, further bending my back, curving me to his body. He moans forcefully in his throat, tormented and lustful, making my thighs squeeze in response to his attention. My whole body reacts like I don't own it; this dream eases me into a sense of false security. My heels leave the ground, and he glides us back into a wall in the darkened room. I don't know where this room is; I can't smell or see; I can only feel.

It began like any other dream. It started with a dinner party, and most businesspeople I knew, including my father, as we collaborated with them. I watched myself as I filed countless pieces of paperwork. So, this became another boring dream, convincing me further that I'd over-worked myself, or so I thought. *Am I so lonely and desperate?*

The man's bulge against my lower stomach told me this was much more, at least I would like it to be. Teasingly, he smirks, instinctively wanting me to draw his lips to my mouth. But he just leaned into my ear and moaned softly as I felt gooseflesh racing along my skin. His hand brushed the hair from my shoulder, and his breath began lightly murmuring in a language I barely recognized. He licks my ear gently, and oh so gently, my body heats up unbearably. I start to pant as his hands find my breast, slipping them up and out from the confines of my sleeveless gown. The cool air touches my nipples, making me whimper. His large hands squeezed them while teasing my nipples.

He is rocking against me, lowering to fit in the crux of my thighs. "Tasting you like this. Oh, how I've waited." He whispers to me with so much longing that my insides clinch as if he were inside me. My back arched as his lips touched the tip of my breast. The heat in me gives way to tiny beads of sweat trickling down my back. Closer and closer, he laps, nips, and sucks. "Mhm," my voice surprises me as his tongue swirls around my areola, titillating me. My hands find their way tangled beneath the lapels of his dinner jacket, feeling his cool skin beneath the soft cotton is a body honed with muscle and agility. He shivered when my hands reached beneath the buttons I'd managed to open. Touching his skin caused him to shiver beneath my fingertips. My cheeks flushed from his reaction when suddenly my nerves jolted as he licked my nipple, pinching it between his lips. His dark voice of approval rumbled in my palms from the depth of his chest. I knew he felt it when my hips lurched toward his own in response to his ministrations.

Suddenly, I could feel his hands moving the dress down my body, chills erupting as he lifted one of my legs, hooking it over his thigh as he propped us up among the walls. I feel redness flush my cheeks as the heat in my body washes through me unbearably again. I linked my hands around his neck. When his fingers ran smoothly down my body, his mouth returned it up to mine, entwining our tongues together; I tasted the faintness of salt with his warm cognac. I sucked his tongue, attempting to take his essence into me. I was drowning in need. My thighs were slick and wet. His fingers found my folds and impatiently but tenderly began to stroke and rub, building me into one big, frayed nerve with my stomach clenched, and my panting became mixed with moans and soft pleas. He refuses me, "I can't wait; you have to cum. I need you; let it go, cum." I felt released in a way that flooded my body with relief and pleasure, unlike anything I had experienced before, but as soon as it began to ebb, I felt a different kind of need filling my body.

His penis entered all at once with a striking pain. I gasped. I was quickly grabbing his jacket lapels in a painful and quiet panic. He stilled and didn't move, and his shoulders had stiffened, his breathing labored. "Breathe and relax." Taking a deep breath, the pain eased a bit. He began to slowly piston into me, kissing me again. He had slowly built the tension back. This passion was gentle and tender, sweet. I looked up again, trying to see his face. His hair was blond, beautifully white, and slicked back from his face in an arched fashion. He had eyes the color of coal and the skin of alabaster cream that framed a complete set of soft pink lips plump from their kissing.

He smirked into my eyes and thrust against me, snapping his pelvis to mine. The pressure inside me began reeling. Panting and moaning, I let my head lull back to the wall and clenched myself around him as my muscles tried sucking him deeper. He became more intense with his thrust, and his cock swelled within me. I might burst; he filled me wholly and completely. I became hot again with a coming orgasm. The man moaned loudly, holding me up entirely, bracing me against the wall. I felt my release pour from between us as he ground his cock deep inside, spilling every last drop into me so thoroughly I could scarcely breathe. I stilled and listened, my fingers and limbs going suddenly numb. What, over already! Abruptly, I saw a shift in my vision; his arms felt lighter, and I began to feel weightless.

"We're out of time again. You're closer to me now. I can feel you when I wake. I will find you, Nimarea."

"What?" I wanted to ask, but no words left my mouth—such an odd end to a dream. The man said nothing but held a sad smile. Then he was gone, my PJs were wet, and my mind was muddled.

CHAPTER ONE

S hutting my eyes against the sunshine, I make my way to the coffee maker in the kitchen. Smelling the bitter-sweet fumes from the automatic brewer brought my sleep-fogged brain to awareness. I'd have to get my butt moving today, Father had a big meeting with a new conglomerate, and notes on the presentation were lying on my desk at the office. I finalized the proofreads for some new clients, and producing the desired tech results was nerve-racking. Showering, moisturizing, a suit, and BEHOLD! On the subway commute, I was outside the door in good old New York City. The smooth rumble of the tracks beneath me and the low energy hum lulled me on the way to work, so my mind wondered about that man's shadowy image that kept nagging me a little. I guess I enjoyed the dream. Those hands.... That mouth. Though stepping off the tracks, I feel a prick to my upper arm as a jacketed individual rushes past me; I check my arm, but there's nothing beneath my black blazer. Shrugging it off, I keep moving.

My stepmother greets me instantly when I arrive at work with a hug and kiss on the cheek. "Good, you're here! Your father is having kittens. You can go ahead and prepare the report upstairs. I went ahead, set out the files, and sent the refreshments for the meeting. Oh, and breakfast for you. Don't argue you're as thin as a soap bubble!"

Cathy, my stepmother, approached my desk, wielding her mighty tablet and a mountain of files. Cathy was slim and dressed in a skirt and frilly blouse, her hair neat and high, looking lovely for a woman near her 60s, not that her age showed, mind you.

Unlike my long hair rolled up in a high and tight business bun and black suit, she was well suited for greetings and people. I dressed as planned in a black pencil skirt, a simple blouse, and a blazer. How fitting. They look at the screens and numbers, not you.

Smiling at her knowingly and shaking my head, I felt for her as my dad's assistant. He could be hard to keep up with, "Yes, ma'am, I love you too. Are you sure you got all that?" I nod toward her stack of work.

"These? Oh, I'm okay, dear. I'll upload it to my PA and let you know if I need anything. "

"Okay, Mom. See you in a bit then. Wish me luck!" I headed upstairs, work in hand. I take a quick drink of coffee, set the room lighting, and begin setting up the terminal along with my notes. I hear the door open, but expecting my dad, I finish my setup and greet him with a warning: "Would it kill you to give Cathy a break? You know she'd overwork herself for you and get sick. I know we're busy, but I'm here too. Depend on me more; that's what I'm here for."

"Duly noted." A voice rich with tenor and subtle baritone notes answered back.

Stunned, I turned to the familiar sound of his voice, which sent shivers up my spine and prickled awareness along the hairs on the back of my neck. But at that moment, my face and brain refused to cooperate; I went blank.

Finally, my mouth caught up enough for a simple thought, "I am so sorry! I'm Nimarea Lars, admin to Mr. Lars." I managed a polite head bow with what I hoped was a gentle smile and not tense, "You must be here from the Envole company; please make yourself comfortable. Mr. Lars will be here soon. Is there anything I can get for you?"

"No, ma'am. I think I am all set now". The man was set with broad shoulders and a lithe waist. He sauntered around the vast, elongated office table to stand near the last open window. Right next to my half-eaten breakfast on the small desk in the corner. He leans his hip on the tabletop and gazes down to the street below, content to watch the world go by. I just seemed to want to watch him, watch them. But, ultimately, I shake my head out of the useless wondering.

Mr. High and Mighty Hip is on My Desk!

His hair looks soft and vivid in color; his face is at a perfect angle, and there seems to be a smile just about to appear on his lips...Despite his intimidating stature, he almost looks soft and vulnerable. Approachable... *I am still staring!* He turns his head to me, meeting me with eyes of darkened coal, and the smile I see there is knowing and full of mirth.

I feel my cheeks heat up, and my face gets hot. I spin around to finish and sit, fighting not to gaze at the man. *Become indifferent. What was I, a monk*? It seems only necessary that my eyes should want to follow the one living thing in the room. However, I wish he'd look at me again. His eyes are just like my dream, de ja vous, maybe? Like framed crystals of black onyx and just as glossy, unlike my own, which appeared black at first glance, it was just a deep brown.

I regained composure when, finally, the man moved from the window, casting his golden locks and dark eyes in shadow, his pale face turning in my direction. In my peripheral, I see the man walk my way and head to the chair in front of me. As he sits down, I look at him with a small apologetic smile, "These first four chairs are reserved for administrators and CEOs; other employees can sit toward the back."

Expecting him to give me my soul back and step away, he

sinks further into the chair. "Okay, thank you, Miss? Lars, was it? " I try not to squeeze my eyes shut against embarrassment when his clear and expressive eyes dart up from the table to mine.

"Yes. I'm sorry. You are the CEO of Envole Corporation. I didn't mean to disrespect you and forget my manners. I am not normally this empty-headed." In my defense, I had been working with this company remotely through correspondence. I'd never seen any of their faces!

Pulling my hand off my chair's armrest, I offer him a handshake. His fingers are smooth and coil around mine softly and firmly. The small skin ship makes the butterflies flip in my stomach, and my breath hitches; I try to hide my reaction. He pulls back his hand, and I am hyper-aware of his palm sliding against mine.

He is way more relaxed than I am. He says, "There's nothing to apologize for. I appreciate you considering my company's interest. I feel this will be a successful and long relationship." He smiled again. "Please, call me Valendrial." He leans back in his chair; his fingers on the table are long, elegant, and well-manicured. He casts impossibly black eyes on me, "It is a pleasure to meet you finally, Miss Lars."

The doors opened, and Pops and his board members, followed by Valendrial's men and women of Envole Corp, entered the room in a swarm. As they exchange greetings, Valendrial Envole gets caught in a conversation with my father, and the meeting begins. Computers clicked away amid my presentation, and I only felt like dying initially, but after years of busting my butt to make it, autopilot took over. By the end, everyone nodded in approval, shared notes, and made plans. My father's tall, stocky frame sits back in his chair, confident and ready. I smiled slightly at him, looking prideful at the old master in his natural habitat.

Valendrial stippled his fingertips thoughtfully yet not

tense. "Good, great. This will be sent to development and research first, however." He looks at my father, next to me. "I have a few more proposals I'd like to send your way now that the preliminary is over. How about dinner, sir? My place?"

Father could never turn down more opportunities to haggle and work, "No, you are our client! My treat. Let my people set up where and when, and we'll celebrate new beginnings and success." Dad slaps his hand on the table, laughing, and shakes Valendrial's hand.

Father rises, and so does the rest of the teams, now clicking and buzzing away with work. I reach for my papers and feel a light hand on my forearm. "You will be there too, of course?"

Blushing a bit and drawing back from his warm palm, I straightened the papers to my hip and my other hand at my side, confident and dignified. He may be handsome, but I've been here before.

"If a business is involved, yes, of course. I am Mr. Lars's Chief Executive officer and administrative assistant."

Valendrial smiles broadly. I smile and shake his offered hand, "Till then, I suppose, and thank you. Great job on the presentation!" He brushes my shoulder as I turn around, watching him leave. Sinking back in my chair, I realized how exhausting his energy was! And it was only 10 a.m.!

I realized that I had lost my mind over the day and had pinched myself dozens of times during seven hours of work to ensure I was still living and not dreaming. My dad's house was different in detail in the dream, but yes. There had been a party, check. There had been the hot, sexy, rich boy. Definite yep. *And he strips you of your V-card*! Yes, yeah, there was that. After fighting the images all day, I sat at my desk across from my stepmother; she was texting and scheduling emails after lunch. At the same time, I was reading emails and working on some editing when it flashed in my head again. I squeeze my thighs together beneath the desk when I remember those kisses and the tip of his head against my entrance when he first entered me. "It felt too real." I let out a heavy sigh and adjusted myself in my seat.

"You feel all right, Nim. You are flushed. I hope you don't have a fever." I am dazed and blushing at the screen before me when I feel Cathy's chilled fingers on my skin.

"My goodness, you're burning up! I am telling your father, then I'll take you home." She gathered me up and loaded me with my briefcase and purse. I am perplexed.

"What just happened," I murmur in confusion as I trip to the elevator. She practically shoves me in with a quick kiss to the top of my head, telling me to wait for her in the lobby below. I see her saunter off toward my father's office with a walk I would have for a particular nineteen CEO. Well, if I had that kind of confidence.

The city is still bustling despite the late evening lengthening the shadows of the Ash trees planted in circular holes bordered with concrete around the front of my house. *Has the day gone by that fast?* Heading to the oak door, I suddenly feel dizzy, and my arm burns. I don't think much of it since I was too busy to eat breakfast, thanks to a particular gentleman.

I shake it off and make my way in, but right as I unlock the deadbolt, I feel the hairs on the back of my neck prickle. I quickly looked down at the street where Cathy had driven off, and there wasn't anyone standing still or lurking, but I still rushed inside, not hesitating to put the deadbolt back into place. And the puny little 'security' chain into its latch with me safely inside. My heart is racing as I wait to hear if it's my neighbor or something, anything rational to come by. I tried taking deep breaths, calming down enough to realize how paranoid I was. Though still a bit shocked, it could've been the lights; I go in, nodding in validation as I head to the shower. I take a calming breath and exhale slowly, shaking my fingers, rolling my shoulders, and feeling my tension at ease. I must be sicker than I realized. I made it to the small gray couch that had my plush blanket perched invitingly on the armrest; picking up my book on the coffee table in front of me, I picked up where I left off, reading "Canterbury Tales, The Wife of Bath," knowing I wouldn't last much longer staying awake. My consciousness fades, and the ambiance is as heavy as I dream without direction. Images past from work, people's smiles and expressions go by as I glimpse Valendrial's face. Blackened space gives way to a familiar scene: the hall from work. I step forward, glancing around; I am alone. The entrance is empty with its sleek, simple industrial furnishings and high glossed and polished floors of white and steel color scheme. I hear the *elevator ding* behind me and turn to follow it; my movements are slow and sluggish. Facing the elevator, the doors open, with Mr. Envole standing inside. He is wearing a black-on-black ensemble of black buttoned shirt and slacks, the dark attire contrasting his pale complexion and white, blonde hair. The image of him this way is enticing as he stands in the elevator, surrounded by the silver interior and the shining bronze panels. But, when I look at his face, his eyes seem dark; circles encroach around them in fatigue.

When our eyes meet, his expression is sad and tired; he lifts his arm from the elevator support rail palm up, inviting me. I approach him, but he looks behind me, and his expression is tense. I turn to see what he sees; everything goes black, and I fall into an endless pitch of darkness. I feel my body tingle in awareness. I raise my hand to my face, only to jolt and scream when I notice someone sitting beside me. "It's me, honey! It's me, Dad, ssh, honey, ssh!" My mind clears, and my blurry sleep vision makes his face slightly more transparent.

I take a big, deep breath in and let it out. Lifting my hands, I am shaking all over. "You scared the hell out of me, Dad! What are you doing here?"

"When Cathy said you went home early, I wanted to come by and see if you'd like to go to the doctor." *Cathy, that's right, she brought me home.*

I shake my head with the still-clearing fog, get up from the bed, and realize it's well into nighttime, "Wait, where is Mom?" Looking from the window, I can see the Buick, but I can't make her out. I glance at my father, who sits on the edge of the bed, looking at me with a strange expression.

Clearing his throat and standing, he says, "She is down in the car, waiting for us. She wanted to bring medicine and food, but when she mentioned a fever, I told her it's best to have you see a doctor." He sounds legit, but he is agitated. "Need a bag or anything? Let's get going." He clasps his hands, rubbing his palms together unusually.

I try to remain calm. Is something wrong? "I am fine, Dad. Really. It's probably just an allergy thing; you know how I get. You and Mom should head home. You have meetings tomorrow and need rest. Besides, you seem short; you, okay?" Something seems off. I don't want to turn my back on him but head to the kitchen for a glass of water. I am on edge, and something is wrong with me; I'm still paranoid. Like a prickling of alertness, I want to jump out of my skin at the next noise.

Grabbing a glass from the cabinet and turning to the sink, I see my dad standing in the entryway to my kitchen; it's almost enough for me to jump in surprise at his quiet steps. Dressed in his grey suit from the meeting, his appearance is neat, with the same black signature hair as mine; he wore his hair short folded neatly back, the ends sweeping the tips of his ears with a distinguished grey stripe throughout. My father bore a handsome presence, with a goatee and muscle to fit his broad physique. Standing with his hands in his pockets, he leaned against the kitchen entry's frame, watching me with an unblinking expression, like a wolf eyeing a rabbit, pretending to be docile and pleasing. It sets me further on edge, "Why don't you come with your mother and me? If you don't want to go, at least come down and tell her so. So, she'll see you're well enough and won't worry." His tone is not as suggestive as the words would sound.

"What is this? Why are you pushing me? I said I'm okay. Just tell Mom I'll call her in the morning." I am leaning on the counter with my arms crossed; looking at him, I try to rationalize my anxiety. My defensive attitude works, and I see his shoulders slump and his face drop some of its edge.

"Okay, it's me. I am worried. I push you too hard. Maybe just dinner so I know you ate well." Putting his hands out and open, he palmed.

Now, he sounded more like himself. I feel wrong for not trusting him, "Sorry, Dad. I'm fine, but yeah, I could eat."

Wearing a white cotton top and bottoms, I felt as bothered and frustrated as anyone in a pushy situation but hungry. I'm not 'on the clock to impress.' Grabbing shoes on the way to the door, Dad follows me and asks, "So, what does the best Administrator in the world want for dinner?"

I giggle as we get to the door, and I throw on my jacket, leaving my dark hair loose around my waist. I consider my options, "I don't mind where," something occurs to me then, "Wait, I locked this. Dad, how did you get in the apartment?" Staring at the deadbolt still in place and the chain latch to the door still secured from my earlier freak-out. I hear a deep sigh, and before I can turn around. The world around me goes dark. "Sorry, this will only sting for a minute." Sometime later, I felt my body being moved; I felt hot and uncomfortable. Feeling as though I were floating, my confusion was so heavy that I could only register a faint stinging in my neck.

"Now get her on the plane, stick her in there with that vampire. Then, they set up a meeting with the witch. We'll leave out in the next three days to Toiseach ."

CHAPTER TWO

I woke up on a stone floor, the cold on my cheek making me shiver at the sudden coolness against my burning skin; its intensity increased tenfold. It was darker than a coal mine and just as cold. I feel a wall behind me and push myself against it, trying to melt into it. My heart is hammering like jackrabbits as I strain my hearing beyond my pulse; what *just happened? Where am I?* I couldn't remember anything. There were no faces or voices beyond my father's, which was the most disturbing. What is he going to do?

"You're awake. Just try to be calm, all right? Are you hurt anywhere?" Upon hearing a voice from so near me, I jolted, clinging tighter to the wall. I scan the darkness, my eyes refusing to adjust. Only then did I notice the tears pouring down my cheeks, clinging to my chin and dropping to the top of my cotton shirt? Terror stripped me of courage, but I whispered, "Wh-whose there?" Afraid to provoke the voice on the other side of the blackened room. I try to steady my shaking hands and trembling body. I panicked, unprepared for a fight or flight scenario, "I'm not going to hurt you. Try to calm down. It's me, Nimarea. Valendrial Envole."

That voice dawns on me, and in a shocked, harsh whisper, I gasp, "Mr. Envole? What are you doing here? Where are we?" My head swam slightly, and the darkness made my vision feel dizzy and distorted. I straighten further against the wall, curling my knees up to me; I shiver but feel myself burning simultaneously. I hear Valendrial rustle beside me and place his hand on my forehead, "You are reacting to something. They drugged you to smuggle you here. I'm sorry there isn't anything I can give you to help." I pulled back with a hint of apprehension, still not knowing his involvement.

"Mhmm, it must be something like Sumatriptan, maybe. I'm allergic. I think my father did this to me. No, I'm sure he did, but why?" My throat feels hoarse; my hands rub the cotton of my shirt in an attempt at self-comfort. I was overwhelmed, clammy, and anxious.

"I'm sure we can figure something out, okay?" He whispers; in this close and quiet space, it sounds close to my ear.

"Do you think we can escape from here?" I ask.

A sigh is all he can provide. I feel him settle in beside me, not completely relaxed; sitting beside me, we settle on the cold, hard floor. He is cooler to the touch than my feverish warmth. My heart feels like it's breaking from the turmoil and stress. *What happens now?* My heart felt as though it was hammering all over the place. My emotions swarmed. I let silent tears fall, my trepidation and pain: all my confusion and hurt bare. I don't know how long we stayed like this, my silent grief racking my nerves before we saw the light come on from under the door to the darkroom, illuminating the stone-tiled floor. Revealing the windowless room, I needed to familiarize myself with it. *Where were we?* I shook my head. I feel like I'm mad in the head. *How could my father do something like this?*

My head spins slightly, lifting it off the wall as Valendrial faces our company. I try to stand using the wall behind me. I attempt to step forward, but Valendrial steps ahead, blocking most of me from the other side of the door. Four men rush in fast, making me back into the corner away from the struggle as they surround Valendrial; he gives two of them solid connections of fists to the face as the third hits Valendrial over the head with the butt of a gun, stunning him. The two collect themselves quickly and pin him to the ground. Valendrial's eyes meet mine, and he registers the shock on my face; he pushes against the hands that bound him to the floor. The gun is pressed against his neck, injecting him with something, as the firearm gives an audible pop. The violence of it all leaves me shaking and tearful. I glance at the door, tears falling, unblinking, and the fourth man stands watching with a sneer as he heads in my direction. Valendrial starts fighting more violently, thrashing around, "No! No! Don't you touch her!" I back up to the wall, shaking my head 'no' at the man ardently, heart hammering for thought or direction. I reach out to smack him away, and he catches my arm and slams a hand into my chest. I hear a deep male growling as the wind is knocked out of me and what could only be more scuffling from the floor. The man keeps his hand to my throat and begins to choke me out. Everything is tunneled, seeing speckles of black dots in the dimly lit room. My breath leaves its lungs as if evicted. My feet are kicking and sliding across the floor, and my hands are clawing and scratching; he laughs. I'll never forget that laugh and his eyes as they looked at me, full of excitement, domination, and evil. I feel burning under my skin as he frees a hand to reach for a syringe and spears it into a space above his other hand that is still applying pressure. My legs are flailing against him to no end without any effect as my arm becomes bruised and battered from trying to remove his hands from my neck. Just as I began to blackout and weaken, I had the last glimpse of him raising a hand high in the air behind him. I feel a resounding smack to the side of my face as I am promptly left to crumple to the floor, gasping, dry heaving, and seeing more than stars. My heart goes into overdrive, and my vision turns black.

"Dosed them enough so the bitch won't wake up until the boss finishes his deal." The bastard snarls.

"Nimarea!" Valendrial growls out her name, his voice filled with rage as he surges against the three piling on him. The distraction caused by the man who hit Nimarea causes them to get thrown off balance. Shifting his weight, he throws the top bastard off, ramming a foot to the knee of the man to his left; Valendrial doesn't stop to watch him grip his leg in a screaming fit of pain. The two left unharmed attempt to jump back on him, but he ducks low and runs into one of the two men, shoving him into a wall; the man attempts to reach down and yank Valendrial's hair, but only results in Valendrial flowing his momentum upward head butting him in the nose. The last man that held Valendrial on the ground grabs him from behind, trying to pin his arms and pull him, so Valendrial counterbalances him and throws him over his shoulder on top of the broken nose victim and then kicks him downward in the face.

❋ ❋ ❋

She went down hard; Valendrial saw it and could not stop it. Looking down at Nimarea, he found copious rage filling him, seeing her fright-ridden face. Those bastards had hit her. No, one did. "Well, that's all of them. Except you." Valendrial grins at the man writhing in pain. As Valendrial brings the person forward, the room grows dark and hazy, so all that is left in the man's vision is the vampiric devil himself. He pins the henchman to the ground using his knees to pin their legs; grabbing the knife from the belt at their thigh, he brings it down quickly into the hand that hit her. Due to the man's nose being broken, he could only render a gurgling wail, and his eyes rolled. Valendrial shakes him, "Bet this feels better than a backhand to the face, yeah? Where are we, and which way is the exit?"

Through gritted teeth and fear, the man answered, "Northwest point through the forest leads to a pass between the hills—" Valendrial would have to take that information and figure it out as they went. Continuing to look at this guy's face shortened his last string of patience when he pictured her frightened face and the snap of his hand on her skin. Despite the heavy dose of sustainers they had put into his system, Valendrial felt the call of his magic and power pushing through to the surface. His veins began to sluggishly pump magic throughout his body, causing his veins to blacken along his skin like spilled ink on a waxed table. Valendrial's eyes dilated, his vision sharpening to widen the spectrum. His fangs elongated for the strike; the man sensed his impending death like a hollowed-out hallway. Everything faded except his breathing, the severe inhaling of frosted autumn air in the dusty, stoned basement. Fear was what he knew when he left this world: terror and darkness.

Valendrial dumps the corpse, the only one he killed, and feels that tightening pull on his heartstrings when he walks over to the bodies and sees Nimarea lying there. She's all he has ever genuinely craved for in all his long existence, and he couldn't protect her. Gingerly, he picks her up, laying her body across his chest, her head nestled in the crook of his neck. Her face is swollen, and bruising is showing on her abused and reddened skin. His moment of getting to hold her, and he has to do so in failure. Valendrial takes a deep breath, shaking off his regret and self-loathing. He begins to feel the rush of power being more challenging to reach and an impending hunger for blood rise in the pit of his stomach, charging to a nearby stairwell in the stark grey-and-white facility. He strains his hearing for any conversation or footsteps around the corner, trying to make as little noise as possible. Picking up nothing, he determined to hurry. The fever was spiking in Nimarea, and she was only getting worse. Thanks to dulled senses, Valendrial hears voices behind him, unsure of where they are coming from. Not giving any more thought, he stuck to one side of the stairs and tried to keep fast and low as much as possible so that he could peek over the top as he reached it to avoid any more surprises. The shouts became louder as a Valendrial could hear the group split to look for them, making his steps more hurried and his heart hammering. Seeing an empty corridor, this landing was more of an inner balcony with rich wooden varnish on the floor and what could be twilight or dawn, peaking through the gauzy cream curtains toward the front building. Valendrial stuck to the wall, edging around the squared landing and down the next flight of steps. Westward, the soldier had told him, he'd have to figure that out once they were out of here. A kitchen cook screamed as he burst down the door. Backing away from him, the cook ran out the side door, hiding in what he presumed was the dining hall. *I need the exit*! He saw past the granite countertops and dangling cookware, glass doors leading to straight woods as angry shouts became closer and footsteps louder. Quickly, snatching a loaf of bread with the hand and arm supporting Nimarea's legs, Valendrial used his other hand and body weight to slide the door open and run out of the building. Not bothering to look back, he focused on going forward, keeping an eye out for any traps or uneven ground. He was no fool of the human ability to track, and if those guys knew their stuff, there didn't need to be any chances taken. He wasn't familiar with the location, but the kidnapper had said 'pass,' which meant there was a risky chance of one way in and out. It could be a private pass. All he could hope to find was a vantage point and figure out the next part. First, he had to gain distance and find cover; it was twilight, and he could handle it alone, but not with a sick human. He could get her healed enough because it was safer to travel at night. He hurried as fast as possible, using what light was left to put as much distance between them and her father's men.

After some time, he hadn't heard the distant shouts of humans, and he didn't smell any dogs, which was a plus. Or was it? Something seemed wrong. He couldn't risk counting on the small hopes, taking shelter amongst a slanted shelf of earth. It was a bit of a crevasse with significant growth of leaf coverings over the earth and rock that made up the walls. He knew it was a risk, but it was the best hideout he could manage with Nimarea so sick. Setting her down gently, her face twisted in discomfort, coming to just as he covered the tops with makeshift branches he was gathering from outside their hiding place. He moved like this for three days or more, tending to Nimarea's feverish body.

CHAPTER THREE

I heard leafy rustling and felt cool leaves pressed against my back. My body ached all over, the heat was unbearable, and the excellent ground caused me to shiver. Sitting up slowly, I see Valendrial rummaging with the leaves of what looked to be a low makeshift tent against a large bass tree. "Where are we? How'd we get out?" I start to stand, and I feel my legs shake. I place my hands on my thighs and take a deep, cleansing breath, breathing in the deep-scented forest of earth and wood. Standing fully and shaking, I sighed and glanced up at Valendrial. He has a slight smile on his face, watching me. "It's good to see you gain consciousness. Still, you should take it slow, okay? You've been in and out for three days." He crouches down next to me; taking my hand gently, he leads me out of the hastily built structure of leaves at the base of a vast tree and to a slate rock and muddy hillside. Brushing back the plant life, he reveals a slight trickling of water running down the rocks and disappearing into another small crevasse below, "It's best not to drink too fast."

"Thank you," I say before turning to him, sincerely looking at him for the first time since coming out of that dark room. "You saved my life and went through a lot to do so. I'm so incredibly grateful." Here he was, the CEO of Envole Corporation, saving lives and ruffing it after a horrible kidnapping. I can't feel appropriate emotion for what we've been through. There was darkness here, yet the moon gave us light through the canopy. I saw the beauty in his dark eyes shining with that little bit of light, like stars. The night graced his stark snow-like skin, coming alive under the night's depth.

As if he feels my emotional instability, he explains, "When

you got hit," He paused, his jaw clenching tightly in anger, "I took advantage of the moment and fought us a way out of the room—then tried to rest of the way hurriedly. I'm afraid we'll have to keep moving, in any case. At first, I didn't think they had been doing much tracking," he pauses, scrunching his brows, "But I think they have wolves." He states quietly, making the eternity found in the night stretch like the uncertainty of our circumstances.

I take a drink and sit down again. My muscles are protesting, but I do my best to stretch out the kinks. The water helps to clear my head, and the fevering heat begins to subside. "Where are we going from here?"

"We should keep heading northwest along this hillside. There's a pass ahead leading out of the valley." I watched as Valendrial fixed the makeshift roof and made us some rather comfy pallets to sleep on—made of sizeable leafy foliage for a cover over piles of dense moss and dry leaves. Valendrial went out again, and when he came back, I was getting cozy on the pallet nestled in the cool leaves against my waning fever, "I am going to try and catch us something to eat. Berries, hell, anything I can manage. Here, have this bread. I managed to snag it from the kitchen on the way out the back. It's a bit hard, I'm afraid."

Handing me the loaf of hardened bread, I paused in my attempt at a respite, "You think on your feet. Thank you. What about you? Here, take half." He looks down at my outstretched hand, holding the bread between us, "No, you go ahead. I'm sure I'll find something." Looking up from the makeshift nest he built for me, I get a good look at his features and notice his eyes are reflective. Like a cat with that tapetum lucidum tissue. *What in the hell did they drug him with?* I ask myself, but I don't dare say anything out loud. It could be me, after all, simply hallucinating. Trying to shrug it off due to my drugged system being out of whack, I ask, "Do you need help with anything? I'm new to this survival stuff, but if you give me a job, I'll see it done".

He smiles softly; it reminds me of him in the office that morning, leaning on the window, so content and happy. I feel an overwhelming sense of the time I lost. How long ago was that? How long have I been here? He responds with certainty, "Of that, I have no doubt. We're good, in any case. Hunting without supplies is just sitting and waiting. Rest, I'll be back soon. If you hear anything, head left from this tree and then northwest. If we get split up, we can meet up there." I got the idea but wanted to avoid getting separated. I tuck in further and listen to the sounds of Valendrial's steps growing faint. The sounds of the night were calm and peaceful. The sky breaking through the tree line illuminates the ground in front of the makeshift shelter Valendrial built. I don't know how much time has passed, and I was unaware of when I drifted off, but I find myself waking up; opening my eyes, I see a pair of dark pants against an even darker forest backdrop. My heart is hammering in my chest as maybe they caught up with us, and Valendrial hasn't returned. But before I can stress anymore, I hear a transparent, "It's me, don't worry." I immediately feel a rush of air leave my body, though my heart is jackhammering. He drops beside me and hands me a couple of leaves full of small chunks of roasted meat and berries. I take to it ravenously. I asked between bites, "How did you manage a whole deer? Won't they be able to track you?"

"As I said, traps and sitting and waiting. You do realize I was gone for over two hours, at best. Plenty of time to make scarce any tracks I made." Wide-eyed and cheeks full, I shake my head. Laughing, he gives that boyish duck of his head. Looking ahead, he casually points an index finger. "Gathered the water from a small river nearby in this discarded plastic jug, so drink plenty." I look at the mug suspiciously but make no argument. Valendrial smirked, seeing my distrust of the mug. Swallowing, I had to ask, "Any idea where we might be?" *Get his mind off that jug!* Valendrial shakes his head, and a frown appears," 'Fraid not. I managed to grab shady directions from the guy who hit you before getting us out. I hate it, but it's the best we've got."

Nodding my head solemnly, I try not to recall that man's face, "A plan as good as any. Well, until we starve to death."

"Hey, give me some props! I managed that, didn't I?" I laughed as he looked feinted, being affronted. He smiles but continues, "We have to travel light, though that protein will help to get your strength up; I'm afraid this might be the most cordial meal we get from here. I overcooked the thinner bits to hopefully dry enough for later, though," He pointed to the small hunks of meat portions of roasted deer in front of us.

Smiling despite myself, I slowed to nibble my food, trying to figure this guy out, "I'm beyond grateful. What you've managed is amazing. How did you get so good at this stuff, being the CEO of a company? You know your way around the woods."

Placing a hand under his chin in thought was done gracefully, unbefitting our circumstances, "I wasn't always a CEO; I did my time in the jungles and forest. I like living rustic occasionally to remind me of the time that has passed in this world and how far it's come. But yes. I learned enough to get by".

"Sounds like you've got a past story there," I say quietly, not wanting to pry.

"Yeah, but don't we all." He says this while leaning against the wall, exhaustion eating at his Features. He gives me a side glance, "You should rest some more. We're going to need to get moving soon." Giving him an affirmative, I nestled back in for a rest.

It only felt like I was asleep for a moment, the odd smell

of antiseptic in my nose and sluggish feeling hard to ignore as we moved out quickly, dismantling and covering whatever signs of life we had made to the best of our ability. I was continuing away from the building that housed my lunatic father's goons. It had been a few days since Valendrial fought for our freedom. The second day, we heard distant shouts and coordination tossed around; they meant something to Valendrial, but that also meant we had to hightail it day and night to get some distance back. We headed the same path as the river but further from it to keep away from visible points. We found another stopping point, and this time, I was good on my word and helped Valendrial set up a camouflaged hut against some trees in a dense corner; our backs at least afforded some cover.

Setting down our small reserve of supplies we gathered along the way, Valendrial spoke out our next moves as if airing out his thoughts, "Set down early, head out the minute it gets dark. I think we're getting close; we'll know by night. But the air is getting denser".

"I hope you're onto something there," I say to him, sitting down, stretching, and releasing the tension in my aching muscles. It had been another day, but I still felt sluggish and weak.

"I'll do a quick scout around. Then can you take a second watch?" Nodding to him, he stalks off into the brighter afternoon. I watched his form leave, and just like that, he was gone. He was a relief to be around; his assuredness and capabilities were astounding. I would be dead without him or still captured. The forest's peace was lost in the chase for survival as exhaustion started in full force, but Valendrial put up with it all. His resolve to overcome this became my fire as well.

❋ ❋ ❋

After that day, I went to wash in the river and found purple bruising from the attack with the guy in the darkened room. I burst into tears at the vivid memory, and for a moment, that walk of fired resolve I had built crumbled. Valendrial had walked precariously into the water and gently took my hand. My hair was drenched over my shoulder; my tears became part of the flowing river. His warm hand reassured me that I wasn't alone as crazy as things had gotten. He'd been there holding me through all of it for no reason other than being decent. I grew to respect him, but more questions began to arise as we spent time together. What did my father want from him? Why were they drugging us, and what with? Valendrial seems vague about his past. While I respected him, I still had a lot I didn't understand or know. The things about my father were the biggest mystery of all. However, we were easily compatible, sharing jobs or watches during the day so the other could get rest. We trusted each other due to the instinct of survival and began to grasp the basics of each other's character, but those little things still wanted to nag at me.

CHAPTER FOUR

Suddenly, Valendrial moved fast and down low, signaling me to his right. "Time to move." Around the fourth day or so, I began to lose count. My nights and days were so thrown off, and the people hunting us were getting desperate, "We must be getting close to a town or something." I whispered harshly with irritation as we tried to move swiftly and silently.

"Agreed." And sure enough, as our steps became more prominent, we noticed a driven path through cutting in the middle of the forest to the left, "Fuck's sake, a path!" Valendrial's voice was full of relief, as were my nerves. Turning swiftly, we fly through the narrowed tree line. I keep hauling my feet as fast as they would go, but I am slowing Valendrial down. "Keep going; you can do it, Nimarea. Go!" I heard him yell at me. My lungs are burning, and my limbs are numb. The shouts are a bit fainter. But then we burst through a road with a mountain in front of us. We had made it to the pass the soldier mentioned!

But where the hell do we go from here, "Val?" I look at him, gasping, arms raised with my hands on my head, trying to catch my breath with burning hot air scraping my throat. His porcelain skin is red and flushed, glistening with dew drops of sweat. A truck, a tiny old beat-up model full of seed and feed, comes by. Without thought, I reached out, flagging down the driver in frantic waves, standing directly in front of his truck. Swerving to miss me, he stopped and looked out of his window back at us. I keep screaming to him help us, please! "Help, please. We're being kidnapped! We don't want to hurt you. We need a ride. We need help!" I say with my hands, gesturing and pointing. He is asking us questions, waving his arms as if to move us off the road in a foreign dialect I am unfamiliar with. Valendrial grasps it and begins to speak with him. I caught the words consulate and police. They seem to argue for a moment, but reluctantly, the man consents, and his arm waves at us to climb in.

CHAPTER FIVE

We ended up at the man's farm just outside of the city. I am still trying to figure out where we are. The man's dialect is a miss on me but still somewhat familiar. He ushers us inside, and Valendrial is immediately shown the phone. The man's family came out full—young men, women, children, to the elders. Curious and cautious, they stayed silent and clustered. I kept my eyes on my feet, not wanting to startle them any further or cause a spot of disrespect. Once Valendrial returns, he speaks to the man, bowing kindly and shaking his hand with gratitude. The man smiles, and the mood in the room lifts as the man hurries to the phone. Once the older man and Valendrial return, and the man addresses his family, they all nod and carry on, and a great relief can be felt lifted across the room.

I am bewildered and unsure what to do, trying not to continually stress my hands together or touch anything with my grubby body. A woman comes to me, the wife, I assume. I smile and bow to her deeply, trying to convey my thanks. She smiles kindly, takes my hands, leads me to a small washroom, and hands me a soap of jasmine with a touch of zest, some shampoo, and clothes. She gestures to the facilities and exits. The wash down was soul-soothing, with warm water I've only dreamed about these last few days. Valendrial had called his corporate office instead of the police to keep things from getting 'messy' for the family and handsomely compensated them—adding further suspicion to my already troubled mind.

* * *

Breathing deeply for the first time since they'd escaped, Valendrial tried to take stock of what needed to be done next. He managed to call his associates and secure them a rescue; he also managed to transfer money to this family and lie about calling the police. They were in a section of rural Asia. He had recognized the dialect immediately from long ago. He may have to dodge some tricky questions from Miss-Sees-Too-Much, but that was manageable. She was beautifully intelligent, and magic had chosen her. Nimarea's scent called to him to want her, but more than that, she was very aware and sharp. While surviving together, they had grown a mural of respect and trust between them. He had her nickname in mind since the day she eyed him with the first deer he caught. Smirking at the thought of her cynical and guarded nature, Valendrial heard a door open, and she emerged from the toiletry, looking a bit less worn down and heart heavy. He had made sure she wouldn't lose much weight during the process and went through scavenging for the various fruits and mushrooms to keep her nourished. He even managed to find the ginger root and ginseng. Thankfully, the forest was in the fall harvest period. She'd been through enough, but he was impressed at how sure she was handling herself. He was certain she could've managed independently if she had been combatted and survival experienced, but she was still very competent. He was glad to have her near him, her presence helping him to ignore the rush of weird drugs they had flushed him with and keeping him motivated to continue onward. He had been waiting for her for so long. *Would she accept him? What would she think if she learned he wasn't human?*

The farmer and his family gave the pair a bountiful feast of their local dishes and cuisine. He watched Nimarea eat with tears in her eyes, and at first, he thought it was spice but realized that she was crying in thanks. The woman beside her noticed it and gave her a reassuring smile, patting her back. As he excused himself, the man's younger son showed him where the two would be sleeping. Since the room was scarce, they shared a small room in the back. Valendrial thanked the lad most ardently and noticed the soap left behind. Taking the soap, he'd do Nimarea a favor and at least let her rest next to him, smelling a bit less fermented. *Swamp ass is a mother.* Once he returned, he noticed her nestled in already, but by the sound of her breathing, she was not asleep.

"You, okay?" he asked gently.

"Mhm, I am still a bit on edge. I'm scared and uncertain." She should be uncertain. Most humans would be at a loss of where to go with something like this. It was more than a lot to take in.

Sitting beside her, he turned her to her side and drew her before him. "You can always stay with me for a while when we get back." He sounded quiet and reserved, apprehensive of rejection.

She scrunched her blackened eyebrows in thought. Does she know she puckers her lips when she does that? Valendrial watched and listened for her patiently, "I don't know. I need to turn in my father. God, I can't believe I am saying that! What could he have done this for? What in the hell is happening? It's been days, and I still can't process any of it."

My voice dies out in a painful whisper; dipping my head and running my hands over my face, then back through my hair, I breathed a deep burst of jasmine and vanilla, and tears threatened to take over in a moment of self-pity. Valendrial was silent for a long time before quietly saying, "Until we can figure any of this out, why don't you stay with me until we get some solid answers? "I didn't know how to reply, but when I thought about how those men were after him too, maybe it wasn't a bad idea to stick around and see how Valendrial was connected to all of this. *Why were they after him?* I remembered the comforting feeling and wholeness in his arms as he held me in the river and cried. "Yeah, I'd like that," I say to him in the quiet dark of the room.

"Then that settles it. Try and get some decent rest. I'll be right here." Leaning forward suddenly and most naturally, he kisses my forehead. Feeling the heat rise to my face, I watch as he turns on his bed roll and seemingly falls fast asleep. The softness of his lips and tender nonsexual moment fry my emotions, but it is a comfort I appreciate more than I truly realized at that time. Sleep had never come to me so fast. I was exhausted.

CHAPTER SIX

I was stuck in a nightmare that night, seeing that man's maniacal face sneering at me and feeling the harsh hit of his fist on my skin. Suddenly, the scene shifts, and I'm back in the woods, and lights flash wildly through the trees. I feel someone grab me, "Valendrial?" There is no response as the hand pulls me through the dense undergrowth. I stumbled, falling behind. A feeling begins to take over my body, and my skin tingles and stings. The darkness and moonlight are swirling, feeling the hand holding me, pulling, trying to get me to move. I become stoic lying back on the grass; my chest is heaving, and my mind is racing, but somehow my body is lucid and calm. The arm releases me as I lie back. The spinning images stop. I am startled by Valendrial coming into my field of vision, but his eyes are reflective red as by tapetum lucidum tissue. I can't fight him off as he leans close to me, smelling me like an animal, running his face along my jawline; his lips feel like high-quality velvet gliding down the column of my throat until, baring his teeth, I suddenly imagine piercing marks on my skin.

I flail awake, grunting and whimpering; I had been fighting and twisting in my chair at the airport, having dozed off waiting for the clearance to finish on Valendrial's private jet so we could take off. Valendrial is shushing me soothingly and trying to still me, but my heart is trying to process its fight-or-flight response, and shit rockets are exploding! I shake loose from him and begin to breathe again. We look at each other, and our expressions are mixed and shaken. Pretty sure my face resembles a deer in headlights, I take a deep breath and shut my eyes, putting my hand to my chest in a self-soothing manner, "Sorry, just a nightmare." I rush out with a scratchy voice.

"No. No, it's okay. After everything, it's only natural." His hand rubs my back soothingly, "Need some water?"

Feeling my back begins to warm up from the soothing circles he is making with his elegant hands, I blush and croak out, "Yes, please," As he moves to get up, I remember the vile they injected him with. The one that looked like it was filled with blood from one of the freaks that had beat us up and drugged me, too. With the vivid dream of him biting my skin, I shiver involuntarily. He radiates confidence and sexuality; his backside is hypnotizing, sauntering off. He seems otherworldly, and out of nowhere, I think of his eyes shifting in the darkness. "What is that anyway?" I ask suddenly; he whips his head my way, confused.

"What do you mean?" he asks worriedly. My random thoughts blur out before he makes it four steps away. "That thing about your eyes," I feel myself getting animated in my frustrations, "And the fact that the soldiers, mercs, or whatever injected you with that red vile looking like blood. I was drugged, I get it, but something about you and my dad doesn't seem right. What am I caught in the middle of here? Am I fucking losing it? Pretending this shit makes sense." I mumble grumpily, standing up and pacing before I continue to rant, "The police need to hold him accountable, but I want answers, too. Is this something to do with drugs or a cult? Are you a part of a cult?" Looking at Valendrial, his face stares past me, taunt and rage-filled. Before I can ask, I hear an answer to my up-ended question from a moment ago, "Well, sort of," I hear from the other side of the room. I freeze and feel my body tense as I turn to see my father and some of his men standing behind me, uncontrollably, as panic sets in, making my feet and hands go numb—Valendrial moves, placing himself between my father and me. My father is different. Gone is his pacified, loving face that had once told me stories at bedtime. Gone is the sternness of a lecture he used to give during my time of a relatively poor rebellion at the high school prom. Now, all I see standing before me is a man riddled with unrecognizable hatred and anger. I'm emotional and unnerved. I don't know how to process the change in him. I want to feel angry, hurt, and sad all at the same time. How could he do all of this? What do I even say to him?

"See dear, I have been waiting for this since you were born for a few good centuries now," He pauses, smiling at the tense Valendrial, who seemed to barely control himself from pouncing on my father. "You both have a role to play." Lars taunts, flashing a toothy grin. Valendrial waits. He heard the steps coming up from behind them. This situation was not what he expected, and because of his stupidity, they were trapped again. *So, what now? Let's keep this guy rolling the monologue.* Seeing Nimarea start to panic earlier caused his guard to come down. So, he wasn't focused on the crowd around them when Lars and his men approached. He could expose himself to the people and not give a shit about what they would say. Covering his tracks had been easy, but would he lose Nim if she knew what he was? Is this asshole going to reveal everything and cost him his soulmate? His blood boiled, and Valendrial could feel his emotions losing control. Rage battling inside his chest, he speaks. "You're pretty ballsy to show up here." I could practically hear the wheels spinning in Valendrial's head, trying to figure out a way to avoid getting trapped again.

"That's hypocritical of you; I'm touched you weren't as considerate when you stalked my daughter for the last several years." Hathon Lars laughs hysterically as if there is some inside joke.

"I get it; it's all about nuts. Mind getting to the point?" I say, feeling my nerves tighten in my stomach. *What does he mean by years? We've only worked with Envole Corporation this last year.*

His laughter quiets down, and sighing, he looks at me in pity. "You're just like your mother. So, full of fight and determination, you don't even know what you are, do you?" My father looks manic standing there, his broad chest heaving as his large form intimidates the eight feet of space between us and his goons. His dark grey eyes are wide and wild, matching the aged streaks running in the sides of his hair. Lars had, indeed, the marks of a menacing and dangerous lunatic.

"You seem keen on chasing your chosen, and thus feel right into the pit, *Vampire*." he spits the last word with disgust, dragging his hands through his hair, seeming to calm down.

I look at him in confusion, "You mean Valendrial and me? We just met! What are you talking about? Did you do this all because of our meeting at the office?"

"Child, this isn't about his simple attraction to you. His arrival means your mother's empty wish has called you home. It's almost time you learn what that means for us all." He stated, suddenly quiet and somber. Lars rolls his shoulders. "Your mother was special, not just because of her powers as pure-born elven blood, but because of what our bond created. The Council initially knew about us but didn't expect you as a byproduct. A byproduct of two creatures that were gifted by the moon." My lungs caved, and my body burst. I laughed uncontrollably. I laughed until tears streamed down my face.

"Dad, I don't understand any of this," I whisper, beseeching. "My birth mother died in childbirth. Where's Cathy? Where is my stepmother? We can get you some help; you're not yourself anymore. Something is wrong, so please stop this." I say between hiccups and growing hysteria, my hands grasping before me to attempt to hold on to something palpable.

"Cathy, that bag that would have turned you over to the Council had I not married and seduced her, she would've turned you into the Council! They would've taken you away from me! I would have lost everything!" He glares into my eyes; they brighten and shine with an ethereal glow. My lungs are heavy as the hair on the back of my neck prickles with horror and something else I can't describe, almost feral. "You know where she is. Where is she, honey? Where is simple Cathy?" He growls, reverberating in my ear as if he were beside me. Fearfulness spikes, but so does my anger. I feel Valendrial grip on my shoulder, trying to keep me checked because that unknown emotion is the urge to tear his face off. "YOU ARE NOT MY FATHER! WHY? WHY ARE YOU TALKING NONSENSE? YOU'RE INSANE! YOU- "I struck a nerve because his posture became frozen, and he began to shake with rage, though this caved, and for a brief moment, our eyes met, and I see no hint of hurt and sorrow beneath all of this hate and cruelty.

"The stains of belief in your mind, child, rely on the lie. So, feed yourself what you want. We're not human, so better get used to that reality." Lars shifts his eyes to Valendrial once more. Hathon speaks to Valendrial in a dialect I can only describe as a twisted form of Gaelic, but the cadence makes it song-like. Hathon smirked at Valendrial and replied, "See you in Toiseach." Lars nodded to him in passing and moved on from us as if we were acquaintances.

Valendrial turns to hold me in his hands gently; leaning down, he looks me in the eye, assessing if I'm all right. I gaze at him and stare blankly into his swirling black glass pools. I feel a tear slip down my cheek. Ignoring the tickling itch it leaves behind. I begin to weep for my stepmother and the loss of the father I once knew. It was light outside now, and I could hear footsteps all around us as I heard Valendrial giving orders to his men who had shown up. As he guided me to the plane, my head was swimming, and in my grief and confusion, I stayed silent the entire flight back.

CHAPTER SEVEN

"What's in Texas?" It was the destination Valendrial had decided. He looked at me, stunned that I had spoken suddenly, "Well, I have a bit of land there, and we should be safe there until we figure out the next move. Try to hang in there and speak up if you need something, okay? It's an understatement to say this is a lot to take in."

I nod, "Thank you." I can feel my tears glisten on the edge of my eyelids, refusing to fall. My emotions are unstable. He sits across from me in the small but spacious jet; his head turns to gaze out the window. His profile is striking and stands out from my unassuming one. Vampire, what does that mean exactly? Unlike a movie reference, he is here in the daylight, but what then? My father is just a lunatic with money to burn.

It takes several more hours to reach our destination, but we are comfortably escorted as we want to avoid a night's stop; we push until we hit a back road lined with wild brush, hackberry, oak, and cedar. The road is winding and turns with beautiful scenery that is little more than a green blur to me as the car speeds ahead. It slows. Looking up from my lap, I see a small cattle gate to the side of the old, paved road. Just inside, the gate turns the road turns into dirt, leading into a forest of mixed trees and wild growth of thorny rose vines and ferns. My interest was piqued as the SUV surged forward; a second black SUV waiting inside slid in behind us and began to follow as we slowly trudged up to two separate cottages, a large and a smaller one, maybe a two or three-bedroom. Taking a guess, it was for the staff's privacy and comfort.

The car stopped, and everyone began to pile out, with Valendrial giving directions on where stuff was to be put and perimeter checks. I take a refreshing breath of air and grab a sack of groceries, but it gets swiped from me by Valendrial. "Go, get used to the place. Your room is to the right of the living room, down the hall on the left". I hold my hands up, defeated, and he gives me a reassuring smile as I walk to the front door. People are coming and going as I step out of their way. The porch is small and fenced around to the right. In front of the living room window is a small table and chair next to one another, complete with a woven outdoor rug. I couldn't imagine Mr. Business sitting there, but it was a nice, quiet spot amongst the trees and nature.

Getting inside the furnishing perplexed me as well; there were a few Native American art pieces, but for the most part, it was neutral in colors and not overdone in leather, dead bears, or bass hung on the walls, much to my relief. It was cozy with beige, cream, and earth-green cloth couches, with an aged record player lined against the wall. A Smart TV and classic movies and books were stacked on either side of the entertainment center. It felt like a grandfather's cottage. *'What an old-timey guy.'* Not sure how to take this one. The kitchen was more modern but still left a rustic feel, with its wooden cabinets and iron skillets here and there. Turning away, I wanted to see my room—preferably the bed. I was exhausted but didn't want to tell Valendrial; he seemed distracted.

The layout of the place was straightforward. I opened the door, and there stood a beautiful four-poster bed done in dove white sheets and plump, luscious pillows. To the left of the bed lay a bathroom with a full shower and bath amenities. A small walk-in closet was included. A window had been closed with heavy, light grey curtains. In front of the window sat an oak vanity with a faux fur white foot rug beneath the small seat. It was a beautiful room with very light grey touches to the white and oak accents. It was like the sky and forest living amongst the clouds. I felt guilt-ridden about my dirtied clothes and the white sheets, so I gingerly sat at the edge. I wanted to shower but needed to wait for my luggage. We had stopped along the way to buy clothes and things.

* * *

I don't know how much time has passed; however, to my surprise, I wake up to lights shining in my eyes and an older man looking at me professionally. Valendrial is pacing. "She fainted, Val; she did not die. Most likely, it's just exhaustion and emotional distress." The older man stood and sighed, placing his equipment back into his bag, "Help her to the shower and let her rest. If something else comes up or fever, I'll come back." He pulls Valendrial aside and whispers something to him. Valendrial follows the elder to the door, shuts it quietly behind him, and then turns to me with a look of determination, causing a flush to my cheeks.

I shake my head; my hand comes up to meet my temple, feeling a full headache had formed there; alarmed, I ask. "What happened to me?"

He crosses the room to the suitcases and unpacks my things, like pajamas and...underwear! I jump up to snatch them. Something is wrong when he looks at me and then down at the suitcase again, and his face seems dark and gloomy. "I just came around the corner to give you your bag, and you were on the floor as if you fainted. Sorry, it startled me. I didn't mean to intrude on your privacy."

With a non-committal sound, I reassure him, hoping to ease his tension," I'm okay. I was just tired. I'm sure I need a shower and something to eat. I must've slipped to the floor. I didn't want to dirty the bed, so I barely sat on it." Giggling slightly with embarrassment, I cleared my throat to change the subject. "Was that a doctor?"

"Yes, he didn't do more than take your temperature and blood pressure. I didn't know if it was serious. We don't know what your father injected you with or what side effects it could cause." He hands me unzips my toiletry bag. "If you want, we can run a taxology test to determine any traces of it may be left in your system if you continue to feel any side effects."

Nodding my head," Thanks for taking such good care of me. I'll keep it in mind." I say as he nods, stoically removing my unmentionables and other clothing from my luggage. The man is on autopilot! I get up to take over and preserve my dignity, but it is unsteady. Valendrial reaches out to steady me, grabbing my arm and hip. How embarrassing; every muscle I own hurts with my movement. Not only that, but I am fully aware of his hands on my person. "Still, you should probably take this opportunity to get some food before you sleep." Helping me to stand, he releases me, standing at arm's length. "I'll have some pain medicine ready with your food once you bathe. Are you-?" He paused. I look up, and his ears are red as he avoids eye contact. I'm confused by his internal struggle until he says, "Do you need help getting in the bath?"

My face responds, flaming red. I may be sore, but I'm not dying. The pervert in me, though, ah, she's trouble. "I'm good!" My moue of embarrassment is hard to miss. "I got it, promise," I say more calmly.

Making a rough noise in his throat, "I am so sorry. I didn't consider you'd be this worn down. I don't have a female staff member." Walking back to my bags, he handed me some clothing. Taking my bathing soaps and other items to the bathroom, I hear him run a bath. Thinking of sinking into that warm, bubbly water makes me cry. I took way too many things for granted before all of this.

"It's ready for you. I will grab our food, but I'll be here if you need me."

"Valendrial," I squeaked out. "Thank you for everything. I couldn't express my gratitude to you for saving my life and taking good care of me. I'm truly grateful." Looking into his eyes, they soften for a moment, and giving a half smile that says a lot between us, he answers, "You saved me too." He states with a pause before heading toward the door. "Go ahead and soak as long as you want. I'll be right back."

Heading into the bathroom, the bedroom door clicks close as I shut it softly behind me. Placing my cooler palms on my face, I step into the bathroom and notice a small shower in the corner. I decided to rinse off first, then drop into the steaming bubble bath. As the water hit my skin, I felt a prickle of stinging relief after a deep plunge of pneumatic pressure of chaos over the last several days—washing and stepping out of the small shower. Sinking into the warm bath and bubbles, I was reminded of the emotions I had been closing off. And I still felt like the lid was pushing back. I wanted to ignore that feeling and kept taking deep breaths to relieve some of the overwhelming roller coaster that would be. Using Valendrial's image as a distraction, I insert his presence into my mind and blur the rest. There is something desperate in the darkness that breeds way for an even darker passion and confessions of the heart. Perhaps this was my own. I wanted to paint him over with my fingertips, sweeping them through his soft platinum hair. Just as my hand began reaching down my body, I stopped short, snapping out of my direction of thought. *This is wrong.* I recognize that my emotions are incredibly rampant; I need sleep. I came from the bathroom, clothed, dry, and refreshingly relaxed shortly. Valendrial is equally washed and freshly dressed in the room next to the window. He was watching out the window; arms crossed, his stance tense as he stared deeply into the trees. On the bed lies a plate of sliced fruits, meat, and vegetable medley with a glass of iced water and a bottle of pain relievers on the bedside table.

He looks at me, his face dropping the edgy look, and smiles shyly; his depthless dark eyes melt into me. I break away from eye contact and sit gingerly on the bed. "Is there anything you need?" he inquires while walking to my bedside, turning down the covers, and helping me move underneath them.

"I haven't been tucked in since I was a child," I say with a bit of laugh at first, but melancholy sets in, thinking of my stepmother and her gentle smile and kisses upon my brow. Tears prickle my eyes again despite my attempt at control. *But not being human? What does any of this mean? This doesn't feel real.* "I don't feel much like eating."

"I know." He leans to my form as I sit up against the pillows when I feel gentle lips on the side of my temple, and it's just enough to break me. I feel him sit down as his arm wraps the front of my chest and pulls me to him, cradling my head as I weep. Some time after, as the tears subsided, he leaned me back, handing me a tissue to wipe my eyes and nose; he stood and petted my head gently, " Process as little as you can right now, or you'll go into shock. The doctor is still on the grounds, so if you need a sedative, let me know. We'll sort this out together. I'll be just across the hall." And even though he wasn't overly affectionate or swarming with support, it was just right for me. He was perfect.

"Thank you," I spoke softly with a hoarse voice. The click of the door resounded loudly across the quiet bedroom.

CHAPTER EIGHT

"Sorry, I slept so late. It felt more like I skipped a year," I started. I slept all through the night with no weird dreams until mid-afternoon. I felt lighter, and that was a start. The dishes were gone from my room, and so were my old clothes. I could also smell food wafting, making my stomach growl. I had come out of my room to the dining and kitchen area to find Valendrial standing at the counter putting food on plates.

"Don't be. It's what you need. I suspect you have questions."

"Thank you," I laughed shortly, "Do you know me so well already?" I use my hands to comb through my hair; his eyes follow my movements like a cat with a string in the window's reflection. Turning my gaze, I let the truth slip from my heart. "Everything I thought I felt and knew about him was a lie. I loved my father. This is tearing me up inside." I felt him come closer as I sat at the table; he placed the plates beside me. "I just want to hold onto some truth and logic, even if I can't trust anything right now. It's better than nothing. Was anything he said real? Or has he just lost his mind? Did he truly do?" The words are hard to forthcoming, so what was said was softly spoken. "Something to my stepmother?"

He sat listening intently beside me with a chair sideways from the table, his arms perched on his legs as he began, "I don't have many answers. I will put my guys on the ground about your stepmom. We will cover as much as we can to find the truth. Though I never knew your father, I can only speculate about his story. The things he said about your birth and me," he stars at his laced fingers on his lap, considering, perhaps, his choice next, "Hathon was telling the truth. From what my intel has gathered, he is an ancient, powerful werewolf. He and your mother must've been nobles of the court to have attracted the council's attention.

As for me, I was never human."

Never human? What? "So, if you were never human, what does that make you?"

"The first vampire." He adjusts to the table, sipping his glass and eating a grape from his plate. The sight of him eating and drinking despite the dystopian films of bloodthirsty vampires running in my mind was more than a little distracting, "I don't remember my beginning, but I awoke in an abandoned lab in the land your fairy tales call the Fae, Toiseach."

My breathing became more rapid as I tried to swallow this reality at this seemingly unreal change in my reality. There was always a semblance of truth to every story, yet this wasn't the *Bible to Gilgamesh*; these were two very financially influential people telling me they weren't human. That I, myself, was not human. "What do I even ask? We are from a different- realm? Race? What exactly is this kind of place? Where is this place that the government hasn't swooped in and experimented on all of us by now?" I asked, in my best attempt not to overcrowd him with my equally crowded mind.

His face held a contemplative expression, searching for a way to describe what I had never thought to imagine in this reality. "The Majesties of eons ago ruled that humans were too willing to use magic to destroy the boundaries of balance within the world for their comfort gains. Each realm is full of secrets and greed, but their decision was backed by powers humans couldn't fight. Thus, the humans were cast out and made to forget. The doors are sealed except for those who know how to find them. However, who is to know that the governments don't know." He shrugs the last sentence with that same elegance I admire. The silence grew between us as I processed what he was saying. It was as if I were seeing the stars for the first time and being told they were plants all over again. The knowledge is there and acceptable due to the circumstances of Valendrial being in front of me (and very real), but it is hard to fathom.

Valendrial sees my struggle and attempts to pull me back down to Earth. "The Council, if your father is right, will not just hold you there, and I hate to think what they might do to you. I escaped from Toiseach upon my first awakening without spending more than a moment there; my memories of that time are faded and blurred. Either by the magic of the barriers themselves or something else entirely."

My shoulders slump, "Oh." I ate a few bites of food on autopilot.

"But that doesn't mean I don't have connections and can't find out."

"But you just said, even if we get in, the Council might hold me there. What's our plan?" *Focus on the things I can control, Nimarea.*

"We need to know your father's goal. We need information first to avoid taking off to Toiseach and falling into a trap."

"Toiseach." I practice the name, rolling it off my tongue. So, what can I do to help? I want to find out what happened to my stepmother, and I need to stop him from whatever he is planning."

"You'll most likely have to kill or imprison him within the barrier inside Toiseach for eternity." It wasn't a snide reminder but an admission of truth floating between us at the table.

It was a heavy silence as the seriousness of his face testified to the depths this would have to go. Could I bring myself to meet my father's judgment? "But, why get you involved?" I asked, dodging the consequences.

Valendrial placed his fingers gracefully under his chin, narrowing his brows in thought. " Again, nothing on the surface comes to mind. I have walked the earth for so long. I very well could've forgotten. This is where our survey will fill those gaps."

Nodding in agreement, we discussed what information we needed to gather. The conversation lightened, and after a moment, I gained the courage to ask, "Does that mean you have abilities? What does it mean to be a Vampire?"

He gazed down directly into me with eyes the color of dark matter, which grew large and dilated. With the change in his eyes, his face began to take on harsher features. I felt like it was an illusion, but the fear in my chest was real. Valendrial's change was confirmed as my reaction to him. Adrenaline hiked through me, and a sense of surrender and anticipation licked my skin. A flash of heat erupted from my neck, and my core clenched in response to his eyes sinking into my own. The room faded, and I was hyper-aware of the coolness radiating from his body and the smell of the woods at midnight wafting from his skin subtly. The man and beast became the embodiment of the perfect hunter against the sensual human nature. Leaning over me, I feel my back meet my chair as his cold hand passes my peripheral, settling on the chair's headrest. *What is this lulled feeling? When did he move?*

Everything feels as if it slowed. My heartbeat hammers in my head and ears. *Can he hear it?* His strange effect on me immediately filled my senses, my whole being wholly focused on him. As if staring straight through the glass of a windowpane, it feels like he sees everything I have to hide. I am entirely at his mercy. I fear him, and yet, I want him to visit me. Nothing but me. I am greedy and afraid. My hand twitches to touch him, and in an instant, his hand covers my own that is placed on the table. His eyes, inky black pools, hold so much heat that my nipples tingle in response to my excitement. My breath fanning against his lips that were so close only a slip of paper could pass between us. He's not breathing anymore, or it's so shallow I can't feel his breath leaving his body or chest moving, and his skin has greyed, and black lines run where his veins once stood. Valendrial stops moving, motionless. My senses are dull and drowsy, but something profound in me is hyper-aware of all of him.

Like the quiet of an approaching storm, just before the battering winds swipe across the earth, like teeth across my throat. He lowers his head, tilting it to access my neck; I grant him access by lifting my chin. Instead of feeling pain, I hear a deep chuckle and moist lips on my skin, leaving my insides burning. "Being a Vampire is being of the Moon and eternal hunt." I feel his lips press firmly, and then just a touch of silky wetness tentatively touches my skin there. Involuntarily, my back arches into him with an intake of breath, after which he pulls away and stands upright as if time resumes its leisure through space. My eyelids had slipped closed as he gripped the sides of my head so that when I opened them, I saw that he was not laughing but struggling with some inner turmoil. We both stare at one another with differing expressions on our faces. My being is one of desire and embarrassment. I release a breath in a rush, and the spell between us breaks, sending us simultaneously looking away.

He clears his throat, though I wonder if it's just a formality, "I'm sorry, I didn't mean to take it so far." *Bury me!*

Meekly, I shake my head. "I'm fine," I mutter. Collecting my thoughts, I grab my juice and take a long drink. I feel eyes on me again, and my neck, where he kissed me, begins to burn. Changing the subject against my inner pervert's will, I ask, "When my father mentioned my being your chosen, what did he mean?"

Valendrial turned his head, clearing his throat. Suddenly, his ears and neck were red. "Nothing in particular. Perhaps he meant that I chose to protect you?"

I didn't buy it. The term was too specific, but I wasn't overly concerned with being attached to him in some way. Out of my father and Valendrial, right now, my bet for survival lies with Val. Relenting for an answer, I changed topics. "What was the language I heard you use with my father before?"

"It's the most common dialect in Sun Kingdom's capital city, Enoleshole, within Toiseach. It's a mixture of Modern and old English from several races on the mainland after the turn of the empire. Though mostly I've heard the modern form has become most popular these days much to the elation of the Council." Valendrial sounded entertained by that notion.

"Hm, it sounds like an odd lullaby to hear it spoken rather than read," I say, pondering the dialect. I had a hobby of learning to read old English, thinking of my beloved Canterbury Tales at home, still open on my couch.

"You're familiar with Old English?" Nodding, the conversation turns to the more common conversation. He was forthcoming about his past company's business and friendship with Sebastian but less so regarding how he reached out to Lars' Corporation. Valendrial and I finish our food before he continues, "I'll investigate where Sebastian, a werewolf I know, might be keeping himself these days. Maybe we can get someone inside Toiseach to see who Hathon is dealing with. If you feel up to it, you can dig into your father's recent activities. See if anything comes up. Meanwhile, another team will research your stepmom."

"Sebastian? The werewolf?" I raise a quizzical brow.

"His human name. It just stuck these last few centuries," he says nonchalantly, shrugging his shoulders.

Wiping my mouth, I stand from the table. "I feel less helpless," I say to my feet. Thank you. I'll do my best to find what I can." Realizing I couldn't access my documents or files on Hathon Corp, I asked, "Do you have a laptop or computer I can use?"

"Yeah, I'll bring it once we're done here." We removed the dishes and clutter from the table, "Sure, I'll go get it. I still have some things to gather and finish before I leave. Let me know if you need anything. I'll be in my study; it was the door just left of the hall."

"Thank you, but how long will you be gone?" I shake the apprehension from my voice, nervous about being alone here. I need to stand on my own, in any case, so I do my best to control my fingertips, tapping the table's edge.

"At best, two weeks; any longer than that, and we risk putting ourselves in more danger with Hathon." I nodded, and he turned to leave.

CHAPTER NINE

Later that evening, I had dinner with Valendrial. The conversation was good and light. The vampire is a plethora of conversation. Knowing just how to help escape from the seriousness of my thinking mind. I decided to walk around the house; the gentle rush of the trees outside, swaying by the wind, brings me a soothing calm, unlike those nights in the woods. Recalling those woods, I remember how Valnedrial's eyes glowed with odd scintillates and listened intently to the woods to hear the people following us. Was he drinking its blood? I remember him returning washed from the river; we had followed most of his more significant kills but never wanted to eat much of the meat, much like the meals we shared lately. Shaking myself from the questions, I stop near the porch and peer into the deep tenebrosity of the woods beyond me. Speckled light flickered above as the variegated stars and moonlight shone through. I close my eyes and let my mind relax. I don't hold onto problems; instead, I allow them to surface gently and let them go. However, I am suddenly overcome with the awareness of being watched. A sense of panic sets into my pulse. Turning toward the deeper woods, I see a furred creature with snarling large teeth and bloodshot blue eyes strikingly visible present in the depth of blackness of the night, practically bulging out of their sockets. It felt like slow motion as my body turned to the door, my scream not reaching my ears despite my mouth falling open. My heart is pounding as it's within an inch of grabbing me. My reaction feels slowed as my heart hikes in my chest. Suddenly, Valendrial is out the door with three additional men behind him. He is shirtless, with the veins of his transformation prominent on his skin. His figure rushes past me, landing on the intruder's form; both begin ground, rolling, snarling, and punching. The sounds of harsh strikes on flesh and the rustling of leaves hollow out my ears. Red smears paint the blueish-white fur of the creature as they break apart, circling one another as if sizing up for the next attack. It comes in a swift rush from Valendrial as he goes for a lower mid-body tackle, leveling the creature on its back. Its giant wolf-like snout is snapping at Valendrial's neck as their arms are locked together, neither gaining ground until Valendrial catches the top of the animal's maw with his hand, ripping the creature's head back and exposing its neck. Sensing impending defeat, the beast starts to flail his legs, bucking in protest, his other arm desperately trying to hold Valendrial's hand at bay. *I can't watch it!* Turning my head and blocking my ears as best I could, I still hear a sickening, deep crack. The rest is muted by shock. I dare not look, running straight inside my room and slamming the door behind me. Once there, I hit the floor, leaning against my door and shaking.

A brief time later, a presence can be felt at my door. A soft knock vibrates the back of my head sometime after that: "I'm fine, Valendrial. "

I wrapped my arms around my knees and buried my head.

"I'm sorry." That is all he says. I get irrationally angry; leaping from the floor, I throw it open to see him having washed, his skin still wet as his damp hair clings to one eyebrow. He smells of clean soap and is still shirtless. Though his features are back to normal, I can't erase from my mind the look of his transformation and the ink-black veins courting over his body. I feared him, but more than anything, I felt guilty and angry at what I put him through, but also by how little I knew of the world I was once oblivious to.

"Stop saying you're sorry." I moved away from the door, pacing my room while he stood motionless in the hall. "I have caused you nothing but grief being caught up in this mess." Turning to him, I show him my up-turned hands. "And you come here to apologize where I would be dead without you! You have my utmost gratitude, but what the hell is in it for you to help me this much? You just killed that creature, right? I assume that was a werewolf, but it still means you've killed them. Hurting others and risk being hurt because of me and my god-damned father!"

Silence fell on between the two of us. I had turned away but could see him at the door. "Yes, I have killed and fought others, but there is a lot at stake if I do not protect you, Nimarea Lars."

"Enlighten me as to what that means for you, Valendrial, *please*." I clasp my hands together and point them at him pleadingly. He goes silent, not answering. Giving up, I threw up my hands in defeat. "I'm sorry, but I just need something that makes sense. Why risk your life to save my own? If you can't tell me, give me something at least!"

He sighs; again, I swear it's a pretext, "I promise I will find a way and time to tell you, Nimarea. I am just as much of a target of your father as you. It is safer to keep together than to make two easy targets. We talked about this."

"I know." I rubbed my hands down my face and through my hair. "I know. I am just tired of the violence. I thought you would get hurt or worse, and it would've been all my fault." I look down to see his bare feet approach me. Feeling his hand tilt my chin up, I have enough time to register the desire in his eyes before I feel his lips gently touch my own.

Her lips are soft like the softest petals of a fragrant flower blooming on the cusp of spring. She smells of deep, earthy roses. Twining his hand in the base of her inky black hair, he angles her head to capture more of her mouth against his own. Drawing her to him by his hand on her hip, his body becomes a flame with a sense of lust. Her lush body arching and breathlessness were lulling him into blissful insanity. Valendrial feels her tongue's tip come out to tease him, and he can't help but smirk at her neediness. She tries to hide her attraction to him so much that teasing her would be almost cruel if she realized what she did to him. After breakfast, when he sensed her eagerness, he felt her back arch off the chair. All he wanted was to take her to his room and make her pant. Though, like a cold wind, he knew he couldn't. He shouldn't be walking her back to the door, hiking her leg around his hip, and slipping his hand to her supple-. Pulling his head back from her sumptuous mouth, he watched her catch her breath, gripping onto his shoulders as if she were drowning, her eyes dazed with lust and confusion.

"I am sorry. That was poorly timed. I -" Setting me down. My mind is a fog-filled haze. He runs his hands through his hair and lets out a breath before I can speak a word. "You are right to have these concerns, and you deserve answers. I have to leave in the morning. I will be back as soon as I can. We can talk more then, I promise. Please stay with the escorts if you leave the house. I need to know that you'll be safe, please. It's the only way I can-." With that, he abruptly leaves the room.

"The only way he can what?" I ask the room breathlessly.

I hear the shower kick on in the room next door.

CHAPTER TEN

Sigh several days since Valendrial left, and I still barely found any leads on my father, and another headache had begun to settle in my eyes from staring at the computer monitor for hours. I rummaged through my stepmother's files from work and Lars Corp. and found nothing. So far, the information there was sound and dull. I needed to hack my father's account, but would that be too obvious?

I was in the kitchen at the table, reaching for my drinking glass, when I looked over recent personal property purchases Hathon had made on my stepmother's account. Nothing began to stick out as the list of properties mainly for commercial marketing, but then one property stuck out. A large villa in Los Angeles. *Wow, a bit on the nose much?* But what else had come up until now? A whole lot of nothing. I checked further into the bill of sales linked to the property, and sure enough, there was money set aside for heavier security and maintenance. I feel a bit uneasy about how open and obvious this seemed. *Maybe he doesn't expect me to try?* Setting my findings aside, I grab my cell and call Valendrial. He didn't pick up on the first call, so I left a message about what I had found.

❋ ❋ ❋

A few days later, he didn't return my calls or texts. I have more anxiety about where he could be, but his men say he is okay and probably stuck in some mess that Sabastian made. I can't risk waiting the entire two weeks. The werewolf that tried to attack was the last one to show up while Valendrial had been gone, which means their eyes are most likely focused on him and not me. I need to take advantage of this.

Collecting my things that evening in a single backpack, I set out. Valendrial graciously left money for me on a debit card for personal purchases. Since my finances were inaccessible for various reasons. Purchasing the flight in advance helped me to get away quickly. Tiptoeing through the house, I cautiously look through gaps in the curtain to see the guards' locations from the furthest SUV parked in the yard's graveled driveway. Reaching the front door, I take the keys hanging on the key ring from the wall, and I'm struck with a sense of guilt at sneaking like this. I am confident these people will attempt to alleviate my need to do this until Val returns, and that's not getting anywhere. Solidifying my resolve, I turn the doorknob slowly and peek out the crack in the door, trying to see all sides of the porch. I *bolt* when I feel the coast is clear as far as my vision can reach in the darkness. Running on, I slide into the gravel, hearing quick shouts erupt around me in confusion. Upon hearing my name being shouted, my hands finally opened the door, and the first security guard to reach the car ahead of me climbed into his driver's seat. Turning the key quickly, I throw it in reverse and drive backward through the gravel road until I hit the spot wide enough to make a quick reverse and floor it to the main road. When I glance in the rearview mirror, the guard's headlights are a reasonable distance behind me. Gaining space, I drove briefly before noting the Farm to Market Road sign leading me to the northbound interstate merger I needed. It's a good thing I picked an airport a fair distance away. If I lose them here, then there's no way they'll catch up.

I reached the airport two hours later, doing eighty on the highway. I texted Valendrial to let him know I decided to go alone and boarded my plane. Upon landing, I took an Uber to the nearest shopping center and grabbed essentials. Finally arriving at the hotel, I take in the small, stale room with its attempt at neutral comfort. It's distance not too near Lars' Villa. Smiling in self-satisfaction, I celebrate too soon; my phone is ringing. It takes me six rings to answer it. "Nimarea." His voice is more profound than usual and has an edge to it. He is pissed.

Despite myself, I feel excited to have riled the gentle giant. *Am I a masochist?* "I'm upholding my end of our agreement."

"You know I didn't agree to this. Please wait for me. I'll join you there in three days, tops." He pleads with her. His voice strained with frustration and aggression.

"No, Val, please listen. There wasn't a single attack after you left the cabin. They might not even be watching that place and are following you. If you show up, it'll blow my advantage here."

"There is no one following me, Nimarea. Did it ever occur to you that this is what he might have wanted you to think?"

I sigh, agitated, "It occurred to me, yes. But if I don't do this on the possibility that I am right, and you are wrong?"

"Nimarea, please." He said through gritted teeth.

"No. I am going. I promise to call you when I have something or if something goes wrong. Don't show up and blow this."

"Nim!" End call.

Sorry, Mr. Hip on my Desk. I'll be careful.

CHAPTER ELEVEN

My first assignment on the job as a "private detective" was to change my appearance. Not willing to cut long hair, I turned to a few short, colored, and styled wigs from a local hair shop. I attempted to blend in with the staple of the street workers I had seen coming into town on my first evening. If Valendrial only gave me three days, I had to hide from him, too. Well, as best I could with a card trail. Dumping the phone he gave me, I changed to prepaid service, using only Wi-Fi calling via the hotel's hospitality. I also stopped pulling out a few large bills and a small handgun I would need to gain access to the streets near the private road to the villa. Paying a few streetwalkers off to let me stay with them on the block down from the villa gave me access to a week's worth of surveillance. The day-to-day comings and goings of the security, guard shifts, and even a couple of stops Lars' men had made with locals to obtain drugs or weapons on drops. Renting a vehicle and sleeping in it the past few days ensured I could follow them at a safe distance the few times they took off. I managed to get off the street and follow one close enough to track down the weapons dealer. My bag containing multiple changes of dark and ordinary street clothes meant that looking homeless to citizens came with a quick change in an alley or public restroom.

However, during this tailing, I was left to hide in the bushes of the derelict housing district. Busted windows and several reports of bodies being found left the area with an uneasy feeling. I packed the pistol with me and wore my dark clothing. Hiding in the depths of the street corners, I didn't dare come close enough to hear anything or go into any of the possible squatter-filled homes. But, as they exited the building, I took note of the man exchanging the cargo of weapons. I followed him to a bar across town, where he threw money at the bouncer to get in.

Attracting his attention was now a goal. What was Lars doing stockpiling weaponry at such a pace? I must gain the street workers' trust while trailing the weapons deal. I wasn't a cop or FED. Passing them the men who would otherwise bug me for a quickie in their questionable cars became a matter of understanding and mutual agreement through the bribe money. Paying them for their troubles didn't hurt the ones with pimps, either.

Valendrial hadn't shown, and the week had passed quickly; on a particularly rough night, one of the guards came down the street to us and talked it up with one of the girls. I stayed off the side, trying to look distracted and at my phone. When I hear words that kill me inside, "Who's your friend down there?"

"She's new, Marcus. She frightens easy." I'm giggling like it's a joke, but I know Delores is just working on the deal we've made, but this one is persistent.

"So? I think they're more exciting when they're scared." I try to avoid him, but he stalks my way. Making me feel exposed and filthy by the way his eyes survey my short black skirt and wild-printed tube top. I can feel every inch of my skin as if I were naked. If I had a full-body snowsuit, a full-face mask, and tickets on the next flight out, it wouldn't be enough coverage to slacken this feeling. A greasy bastard, he rubs his hand on his chest, grabbing his chin. I try not to let any more apprehension show in my features; it's just edging him on. My hands are on my phone in a white-knuckle grip. My heart wants to implode.

"Hey." He says, attempting to grab my hand over my phone, but Delores is closer and pulls his shoulder, making him stumble into her exposed cleavage, more than certainly grabbing his attention as he looks down at it with a smirk. She is looking at me, and I give her thanks.

"Come on, beast; I'll be your "victim" tonight for a special. Whaddya say?" Glancing back at me again, he seems slightly suspicious, but his smile wins over as he reflects on Delores.

"Yeah, all right, doll." They walk away, but not before Delores has the I owe her look again.

* * *

* * *

Within a week and several thousand dollars later, I had the location of the weapons dealer. I needed to know why so much hardware was flowing into that place. The dealer was just the go-between, but the operator owned a club. Go figure. I painted my face with heavy liner and smoky makeup to alter my features the best I could. In alignment with the outfits I saw on the street, I opted for a simple and standard black dress with heels. The club was lined out the door. My odds of getting in were slim. But bless Delores, who is hugging a man's arm on the curb in front of the club. I catch her eye, and she smiles and waves at me to come to her. Linking arms with her, she looks at her "escort," "This is my friend, Jay. Can she join us?" She says my street name with a wink. Making the man smile, he welcomes me to join them, passing the security with no problem.

Entering the club, the music's bass pounded my heart in time with my nerves. I had been through so much to get this far. I dealt with grubby men and women of all social secs pawing for sex from the dark corners of the world's harsh reality, "unmentionables," who were assumed never to be known if they left this world. It was eye-opening as it was heartbreaking. The secret yet public economy of sex was beyond what I ever wanted to be a part of, and yet here I was in the thick of it, about to ask a weapons dealer for information on behalf of my father. I had learned a lot in a week, how to deal with drug addicts, their sellers, and every type in between, and I was only lucky not to have been slapped around or worse because of Valendrial's money. It kept the leaders away on the fence about how to deal with me if I was a threat. I stayed to myself, kept my nose down, and didn't ask questions; it kept me alive. Until tonight, but by the time they decide to silence me, Jay, with no identity, will be gone. I hoped.

It took a while to break away from the guy who escorted me and Delores. Flirting and rubbing the thighs of his jeans while Delores took the reins made me appreciate her abilities, yet again saving me as my skin began to crawl. I was tossing back a quick shot before I went to the VIP lounge entrance. I noticed the guy I needed was at a bar beside the dance floor. Tampering down my excitement at saving more money, I approach him, taking note that he is alone. I decided to saddle to the dance floor to whirl around, making an inconspicuous glance around the club, ensuring that no one else had eyes on the man other than me. I don't see anyone on the upper level or below. The beat of the music is good, though, as I get trapped in the throng of dancers and partygoers. I approach him, notice the drink he is holding, and ask the bartender to double up, slipping him a hundred.

The weapon dealer notices me and smiles openly, like welcoming an old friend to the table. Smiling back, I sit near him and pray he isn't one of those weird types.

"How's it going?"

"Better now that you're here, gorgeous." He smiles, but it is not threatening or eerie and seems like a general compliment. Smiling in return, I turned on my best dazzling smile, reaching for the drinks the bartender had left us. "I'm so glad I could help. Cheers."

I don't drink my drink and watch him gulp his down. He sets the glass down, and with hazy eyes, he sizes me up and down, focusing on my cleavage and exposed legs. For good measure, I cross them, slipping him a view of my little black panties. He wipes his mouth.

"So, where's your girl?" I nod at the empty black bar stool next to him. The music is drumming loudly, so our heads bob in and away from each other to engage in conversation. The lights of electric blues, greens, and red swing wildly around the stage as the DJ keeps the crowd entertained.

He leans over to me and says, "Right here, beautiful." I laugh, feeling nervous. Then he asks me, "Where's your man?"

I look around as if surprised, then lean in, touching his arm, "I don't have one yet." He seems excited and smiles big. "But more than that, you want to make some money?" I ask.

His face changed to skeptical and then interested, but he stayed silent, so I said, "For information on the Lars purchase." Slipping him some large bills, his face morphed into business-like scrutiny before falling back into an easy smile. He began to count the bills under the bar, hidden and swiftly.

"What do you want to know?" He leans in smiling, pocketing the bills swiftly.

"Bulk of the purchase and why." I lean in to ask.

He takes another drink and leans my way, tucking my hair behind my ear and laughing; he is putting up the act. So, I do so as well, leaning into his hand and giggling with him. His arm comes around my shoulder, and his lips touch my ear, making me stiffen in discomfort, "He bought enough damn artillery to warm up the Cold War.

No one ever says why they're buying, though the word is he is stockpiling for a resistance out East. He hasn't sold a single bit of product but the drugs. No one on the streets can figure out who the man with the cleanest hands got pissed at. Best stay away from that business, sweetheart. I'll pretend this never happened as long as I don't see you again, alright? I'm going to kiss your cheek and leave. Forget my face, and I will do the same for you."

I giggled and nuzzled his fingers at my chin, nodding meekly in character. Continuing the act, the dealer's face smiles back, leaning toward my face, where I turn just in time to receive the said kiss. Smiling as he wobbles away, I keep my smile, glancing around the room and noticing it is all clear. I take my time to drink a few drinks, humming to the music. I make my way out of the club. Once on the street, the air is more breathable, and the sky is clear. With the roads still bustling, I needed to be cautious going back to the hotel. I was also on edge at how smoothly that discussion went. All the information pointed to Lars starting a fight, but with whom. Was Valendrial's people amount to that much of a threat against Lars? I attempted to call Valendrial on my way back, but it went straight to the no-service message. Feeling on edge, I nursed the idea of going inside that Villa for more answers and a way to stop my father.

CHAPTER TWELVE

Valendrial stares at the empty notifications bar of his phone in contemplation. It was open in airplane mode, but no calls had been going through since before the flight to New York. "Damn it." He hears a snickering from the airplane's seat beside him. He throws a hand toward Sabastian and hears a loud *smack* and an "Ouch!" Satisfying his anger a little. People glance in their direction but make no huge note of it.

"You asshole!" Sebastian says, fed up with this pent-up, moody vampire.

"Damn straight, Zadaine! If I weren't here dicking around with you. Nimarea wouldn't be in danger right now. With me halfway across the states!" She wasn't answering her phone to any of his calls. *Was it the signal?*

"Calm down. If Nimarea is your nightmare princess, I'm sure she can handle herself. Besides, I wouldn't have bothered if you didn't need to see this yourself." Sebastian rubs his cheek in mock pain. *Fucker already healed*, Valendrial scoffs at his pity act. "Don't need to remind me, Seb," Sebastian mutters about him hitting like a wuss, knowing Valendrial can hear him very well. Valendrial shakes his head, turning to look out the airplane's window. Two weeks ago, when Valendrial arrived at his home deep in the Casper Mountains of Wyoming after several hours of flight and driving to the mansion, he found Sebastian getting ready to fly to New York due to some intel he received on Valendrial's other problem.

"Sorry, old man, but Larsy-poo can wait. I have a lead to follow in your babies running amuck all over humanity here."

Sebastian, formally known to the old world as Zadaine, said with a pitying shake of his head toward Valendrial after the vampire explained his plight.

"You know who stole my blood?" Shock and stillness registered on the vampire's face as he considered what his friend said. He was stunned that now, of all times, he finally had within his grasp when he needed to be with Nimarea. "What do you know?" he asked impatiently.

It was during his second slumber, the one he could account for and chose to take since his first awakening and leaving Toiseach. Someone had stolen his blood, and with its theft, the spawning of tainted forms of vampires—rampant maddened creatures stalking humans like cattle in the night. Valendrial's mild need for blood looks like a trip to the phlebotomist for a blood test in comparison. It was hard to know his origins and what he was. Valendrial wanted answers and to stop these poor souls' torment.

"Eh, not much," Sebastian waved his hands for Valendrial to wait a minute before the sod started scowling again. "Ugh, my source says they are auctioning some of these creatures off to certain military outfits in a black-market bid in New York. They sell like hotcakes since the damn things can take a hit." At Sebastian's cynicism, Valendrial grimaced at the idea of those people as cannon fodder. "Sorry," Sebastian said, tucking his head in thought but then waving his hand as if to clear the ideas in his mind, "Anyway, there's a chance the one who created them will be there to oversee the sale. See? Ergo, perfect timing, and you're already packed." Lifting his head at an angle, he puts his hands together like a salesman finalizing the deal.

"And if this is a trap?" Val crossed his arms, raising his signature eyebrow. Valendrial only had two weeks to conclude with some information about Lars. Is it a coincidence that Seb found something when he set foot at the airport? Val decided to follow the lead for now.

"Then will kick ass? Duh." Sebastian shrugged his shoulders, throwing a shirt into his duffle bag.

Sighing heavily, "Just one thing. Who's "the source"?" Valendrial watched Sebastian's shoulders stiffen and immediately knew who.

Laughing lowly in disbelief, "You did that to her. I called her for a favor after you took off."

"Shut up. Not now, okay."

Sebastian's chosen was a complex and powerful woman, a descendant of the Chewa County in Africa. As a Makwana or "Mother of Children," she can summon the rain and other forces of a spiritual nature. Though her power is limited when pulling power from Toiseach's wards, she is the one you want on your side if you have to deal with the macabre, but Sebastian left her for complicated reasons, breaking both of them in ways that they still hadn't learned to cope with.

Sebastian looks forlorn and in thought with his bright blue eyes unfocused on the suitcase opened before him. His wavy, chestnut-colored hair had his hand run through it more than once today. His slacks wrinkled, and his shirt. Seb must've been working hard, yet Valendrial knew he wouldn't stop. Seb, no, Zedaine, as he was called then, felt he needed to set this right as he left Valendrial all those centuries, neglecting his resting place in lieu of his problems. Of course, it wasn't Sebastian's fault, and Valendrial never blamed the werewolf. Someone from Toiseach was monitoring Valendrial's every move to get their opportunity.

It was something neither of them had seen coming. Humans dealing with his blood was something that had been quickly escalating and was infecting and influencing more than just the humans infected. His blood began to set irrevocable changes to the human economy, science, and wars. It was his blood and his responsibility. The two felt responsible for the underlying tension in their relationship: guilt at what had come to pass. They were a pair. They were the most unlikely family.

He was sighing heavily in sympathy and guilt for his friend. He walks up and places a hand on his shoulder, bringing him out of his daydream.

"I'm sorry, Seb. I'll stay out of it, but let me know if you need to talk." As he walked out the door, he said, "I'll be waiting in the car."

"Yeah, be right there."

* * *

Arriving at the airport, Valendrial pulled sunglasses out of his welt pocket. While he could walk and move freely in the sunlight, the UVs were more distracting to his photosensors; it strained his vision, which was more evolved to that of a pit viper when he used his magic and blood with his spectrum of color increases. He was a hunter who made to paint the leaves of the forest a night sky with the blood of his prey beneath the soft, incandescent moonlight. He could mask his presence in a crowd despite standing over six feet. Taking the regular airline and leaving his jet helped. No one could tag his arrival through flight terminal data. Making it through the street, the pair make it to a destination near the NY docks. "Kind of cliché' isn't it?" Sebastian remarks, looking across the street of the many buildings with all the flood of activity. The smells of New York always made his nose wrinkle with the smell of concrete and car fuel. It was sensory overload for the wolf, and he slammed his mental walls up to keep his inner beast from crawling under his human skin. Valendrial couldn't agree more with Seb's words as they checked into the hotel room. The busy lobby had the fresh smell of food and humans wafting heavily from the filled first-floor restaurant. Decedent furnishings and piano sat silently in the middle, untouched in solemn grandeur as if time stood still just in that place of marble flooring and bright light streaming from front view windows. The sounds of city life were abundant and precious in the place.

They were surveying the view below their room in the hotel. It was a white, smog-filled shore lined only a few miles out. He looked at each shipment container, contemplating which "merchandise" would be on. "You think there's a portal they use to ship illegal cargo from one to another? There is an economic balance in every darkest way on this planet. These people aren't impervious to it; most are paid to hush about it. A result of twisted fears of humanity when they were all born naked, afraid, and hungry."

Scoff, "A touch of Stoicism? I was asking if we should gather some intel in case it was misleading information, and you go spouting poetry! Do you do this to Nim Nim, too?"

"Excuse me?" Valendrial turns from the hotel's windowed view, "Nim Nim?"

"Yeah, like the sauce?" He shrugged his shoulders as if her new nickname was common knowledge. "Because she has to be saucy to cope with your melancholy." He burst out laughing, heading out of the room. "I'm going to take a gander downstairs; do you want anything, old man?"

"No, and I'm younger than you, idiot." Valendrial attempts to point it out.

But it doesn't work. "We still don't know that. I'll meet you here at sundown; don't draw attention to us."

The click of the door meets Valendrial's ears as he mutters, "Rabid bastard," with a genuine good-natured smile. While it was true, neither knew how long he spent in Toiseach before being found in the human realm. The Toiseach council wasn't something Valendrial was too intimate with. None of Toiseach was familiar to him as a home or place he knew. He spoke the language and learned the goings-on because of Sebastian's hunt for the blood thieves. Sebastian had saved him as a lone wolf stalking the edges of eternity. He and Sebastian were a pack of their own. There hadn't been a reason the council cared about his existence, and the only reason he could think of one now was that Lars had told them about Nimarea being his chosen. Otherwise, they wouldn't be involved with him or the rogue vampires. The council had no love for humans and drove them away. They certainly would care if Valendrial and his hybrid mate made magic babies together.

What did Lars hope to accomplish by selling his daughter to the council? Valendrial knew the man was a lunatic, but the answer seemed just out of reach. Also, Lars Hathon seemed to be in league with the organization that stole his blood. How else were they able to drug him on the doorsteps of his own home, kidnapping him? Nothing of the sort had ever happened like that before, and that feeling of powerlessness had terrified him. It was something he had confided in Sebastian about on the way here. They needed to keep their ears pinned to the ground for any updates on the political situation in Toiseach. With the lack of government in the Moon court, it was highly probable that they were likely dealing with the council, Sun court, or both.

Nimarea and Val's reasons for traveling through this mess may differ, but they both had the same destination. There were many things each of them had discussed and shared regarding her birth, but he shared little of his own life, putting her mental security and comfort during the time of her shock and torment first. If Zadaine's love history taught him anything, keeping secrets was the worst thing he could do to get closer to Nimarea. And it was the one thing he had done from the beginning, out of fear and apprehension. When he reunited with her, he vowed to have an open-book conversation with the woman even if it ended poorly. Nimarea deserved a choice, no more secrets. A call on his phone has him answering before he can read the no-name caller ID tag. "Nimarea?" A dark, sinister laughter made Valendrial grit his teeth in response, his body filling with apprehension. "What do you want, Lars?"

"Do you know anything about the strange little bird flittering around my business stature lately in Los Angeles?" Valendrial felt his body go cold with anxiety but remained silent. A slow grin stretched across Lars' face, smearing the lips of the manic prick on the other end of the phone.

"Thought you might. No worries, she's entirely safe. I have no use in harming either of you, I assure you. I need you alive to see this to the end."

"What is that end goal, exactly? Because I'm losing the plot here, Lars."

"Hold on, where is the fun in skipping to the end of the novel?" There was a pregnant pause between the characters; not a single breath was heard between them. Unlike the young blood he sent to the cabin, an Alpha his age would be one hell of an opponent.

Lars spoke first, "Now that you're in New York let's play a game of catch. You managed to escape capture from my men again, and I promised to let Nimarea go without foul play."

"She's your daughter, you sick bastard." Valendrial could barely reign his rage from crushing the phone in his inking hand. His power was becoming unhinged.

"On your mark. Get set. Go." The phone goes silent. In an instant, the room's window shattered inward with the brute force of three heavy bodies plowing through it. Glass shards flinging every which way into his skin. The three intruding werewolves stand tall and muscled out, flanking him with hard stares. Each sizing their best opportunity to bring him down. Suddenly, a familiar dart casing rushes past his neck, barely grazing him; Valendrial's instincts kick into high gear, and he lunges for the first wolf. Bearing fangs, he punches the wolf's stomach as the other wolf gears up and attaches himself to his back in an attempted choke hold. *Perfect*, Valendrial rolls his eyes. Using the man on his back as a shield from any more possible darts, he grips the third man's arm as it comes from the side with a syringe and forces him to plunge it into the first wolf who'd risen from the floor that he'd punched earlier. Cracking his wrist in the process, the wolf howls in retaliation and goes to bite Valendrial's arm in protest. Valendrial lets go of the wrist and plows a fist to his face, hearing the bones crunch under the pressure. Before the third can get off or pull another syringe, Valendrial grabs his arms and uses him like a backpack to cover his escape out the door. Hearing bullets and other darts hit the walls and furniture around him, he burst through the door to find Sebastian waiting there, decking the guy on his back and pulling Valendrial out of the open doorway.

"Gotta gets the fuck out of here, Val." Sebastian was ever impatient.

"I know, damnit. Go up to go down?" Valendrial, ever navigating exit plans.

"Works in video games." Sebastian offers. So, they both took the stairwell and decided to head to the roof. In their quest for an escape, they don't seem to realize there are only so many ways down in a hotel from the roof. One of them is to fall. The gunfire ceases, and sirens are sounding all over the place.

"Cops." Sebastian

"Yeah?" Valendrial

"Well, we both used an alias, right?" Sebastian

"Yeah." Valendrial

"But we didn't hide our faces." Sebastian

"FUCK! Now the whole city will know we're here." Valendrial

"That's true." Sebastian's on-point observation skills.

"Jump." Valendrial all but ordered. Sebastian looked across to the building next to them. *This motherfu-.*

Shaking his head so adamantly, his flouncy hair could help him achieve flight, "You first, they're after you, not me. Better make sure you get to safety and all." He crossed his arms and gestured to the other building like a realtor trying to sell a house with no doors in a gang-filled neighborhood to a lawyer.

"Argh," Valendrial growls at him, "Come on, Seb!" (No sale

on the house).

"Hell, Val." Sebastian takes off running and leaps. Landing in fluid movement, he performs a body tuck to land. Valendrial hears the smack of the body against concrete, then the inevitable "SHIT FUCK!" Sebastian is now rubbing the hell out of one of his shoulders.

"Yeah, that looked like it hurt," Valendrial says nonchalantly as he turns and looks at the door behind him, swinging open to find the police reaching for their guns. Valendrial bolts, yelling to Sebastian, "Meet you at the usual." Jumping to an opposite building.

He hears from Sebastian, who heads off, "What's the usual!?"

Sometime later, the pair meet up at the "usual place"—the small townhouse of one of their subordinates through Envole Corp. In an apartment on the edge of the bustling city, it was a bit farther from the docks than they'd hoped, but they were grateful to have a moment to stop running.

"Burning off from the cops is easy, but now Mr. Envole of Envole Corporation and his trusty sidekick Sebastian are all over the six o'clock news! What are we gonna do?"

"I got to get back to Nimarea."

"Oh no, not that again. Look, Larsy -poo obviously wants to trap you both, right? The worst he'll do is lock her up. He wouldn't risk his 'big plan.' We still hit the auction and grab some information on the vampires. Lars is likely linked to this; we may learn how." Sebastian pleaded with his hands clasped like a fanboy of a music idol. *Ugh, the way he blinks his eyes.*

"Fine, you're right. For now, I need to tell Nimarea. Maybe convince her to step back and go back to Texas." Patting himself down and realizing...

"You left your phone and passport?" Sebastian looks at him with a raised eyebrow. *Since when did he start doing that*? Sighing before Valendrial can throw out any more brilliant ideas for the two of them to fail, Sebastian says, "I'll call in a favor."

CHAPTER THIRTEEN

"Glad at least one of us remembered to keep their phone on them, right Val?"

"Shut the hell up. How are either of us able to be this stupid? How did you survive all these centuries?"

"I try not to think about it too hard, old boy. This is New York. Not the woods where you can hide out in the bush, sucking on deer to get by. We've always managed to lay low and can scrap when necessary, but cops? Humans? In public? We've never." Sebastian scoffed, shaking his rich brown hair, handing Val a loaded wallet, phone, and a bag of fresh clothes.

They were staying in an apartment on Christopher Street. It was close to the Pier, where the auction would be held in two more days. Calling in with the crew he left with, Nimarea set Valendrial's last threads of patience as he yelled at them for the better part of the call for losing her. Feeling his powers about to explode, he tried again to call her.

He can feel her apprehension to answering. After the sixth ring, she picks up. "Nimarea." Valendrial knows where and that she is already under Lars' radar.

"I'm upholding my end of our agreement." She says with such conviction and self-assuredness. He feels his gut dropping to the pit of his stomach. Could he tell her? Or would that terrify her and put her in more jeopardy?

Torn between what to do, he states, "You know I didn't agree to this. Please wait for me. I'll join you there in three days, tops." He pleads, trying to compress his anger at how out of control the situation has become.

"No, Val, please listen. There wasn't a single attack after you left the cabin. They might not even be watching that place and are following you. If you show up, it'll blow my advantage here."

"There is no one following me, Nimarea. Did it ever occur to you that this is what he might have wanted you to think?" *Think Nimarea, get out of there, love.* Maybe if she went now, Lars would let her return to Texas. *What the fuck is he supposed to do!?*

"It occurred to me, yes. But if I don't do this on the possibility that I am right, and you are wrong?" She sounds as frustrated as Valendrial feels.

"Nimarea, please." He said through gritted teeth.

"No. I am going. I promise to call you when I have something or if something goes wrong. Don't show up and blow this."

"Nim!" End call. "Shit! Sebastian, she's practically right outside his door. I have to get out of here."

Placing a hand on his shoulder, Sebastian reminded him, "You leave now, and he *will* go after her just to ensure your compliance, too. We'll get to her, I swear. Let's just let him guess our next moves for a while, yeah? It'll buy her some time, too."

"Yeah, but now what do we do? We called the PR to clear up the misunderstanding at the hotel. But I can't just sit on my hands while that lunatic tries to capture the woman I love." His voice dies off as he runs a hand through his already mused hair.

"Hey, I still love you!" Sebastian hands Valendrial a pair of large knives with dark brown leather casings engraved with Celtic protection knots. Sebastian shows a predatory grin of sharp canines while fixating his Kusarigama weapon on the back of his belt. "We do what we do best, but this time, no humans."

"That shit was a disaster." Valendrial laughed.

"You think? We looked like a pair of clueless asses up there! I'm going to rest for a while, Val. I suggest you rest in whatever way that doesn't involve five hundred years." Scoffing lightly at Sebastian. Valendrial hears the door to the bedroom from the dining room click close down the hall.

Thinking back on the march of time, years after his awakening, he remembered the smell of the city and the number of people that had populated the area since his slumbering began. All the smells and sounds were overwhelming. The changes over the decades happened fast. Valendrial would stick to a habit of dipping in and out of meditative periods of rest to keep from connecting with mortals with whom mortality guided.

He remembers the first time he had felt Nimarea's presence. For the first time in all his lonely existence, he had never known a feeling of such hunger and attraction. He followed her like a hound, his senses leaving him and thinking of nothing else. He stared at her from across the seminar's assembly room with incessant panic. His loneliness drives him to seek her out among the crowd. Despite the risk of her being a mortal, it didn't matter. He just needed her.

Empty, he realized how empty he had been and how incomplete his being felt. As if the slumber was to ebb the half of whom he was into blackened oblivion. Never again, his heart cried. Hopeful and begging.

Coming to a halt, he saw her from the room. Her buttery-like brown skin caught the light like a glowing honeyed goddess. Her hair fluttered in black waves to the middle of her back. Her eyes, her smile. But her short stature, full thighs, and swaying hips made him appreciate the creature behind her creation. She's perfect. From then on, it was willpower, a driving force to meet, love, and worship her every breath. There, in the darkness of night, he fought with that desire which had overwhelmed his instincts, and in the darkness of the night, he found her in his meditations, devouring her in absolute passion. Speaking to her, his lustful whispers in the dark. She had received him and called out as if she were indeed there. It was the most frustrating tonic that soothed his magic upon awakening. It deepened the hunt in his veins.

Valendrial had a chance to observe and learn about her in the woods. Seeing her conquer her emotions in such conditions, her strength. He admired her from the start, her kinky attitude and readable face. She was a bit of a pervert, but he loved that she craved him as much as he did her. In the woods, she was considerate, reserved, and tired but never gave up on the troubles they faced. Always willing to lend a hand. Crying or not, she held on and kept pushing. He wholeheartedly missed her. Kissing her in the flesh was something electrifying, and he couldn't wait to do it again. *By the Celestial Sun and Moon, let her be safe.*

The night gave way to demons. Wild vampires clawed the cages like rabid beasts, gnawing their maws at the bidders flowing in and out of the curtained cargo hold—a makeshift hold was made for previewing the merchandise. Tall, white-clothed tables graced the floor; the waitpersons paid for service, and silence walked the floor with trays of colored drinks and cocktails. Glittering glamour covered the faces of the Fae people here tonight, and the humans wore masks. Lines of people checked the silent auction tables regularly while others watched the show excitedly, waiting for their last chance to strike a final winning bid. Growls and wails are barely covered by the string quartet in a macabre scene of scarcely contained chaos in the form of pure death.

* * *

They were all spiked with the smell of adrenaline, and to Valendrial, it was a heady perfume that teased him of a midnight hunt with the scent of pine and blood beneath a glittering moon of white-blue light. However, his control was above the human hybrids hissing under the makeshift tarp. Their scent was a heady brew, but the sight of pretentious, greedy, blackened, soulless faces put him off. His taste was more toward the thick thighed, shy-smile nature, secret pervert, Miss-Sees-Too-Much. The thought of her making him smile, Sebastian nudges his side, using his head to point to an exciting pair of un-glamoured Fae folk who stood out amongst the rest in the traditional Toiseach attire of the Sun King court. Dressed in harem pants, the colors of fire and gold, their chest was clothed in deep golden silk, the sash around each a patterned color of red leaves, representing the clan the pair reigned from. However, there was a significant difference in the pair's appearance. The taller fellow of deep bronze skin and a head full of dark curly hair was dressed more richly than his short female counterpart, who seemed to be sporting a particular pair of wrist cuffs.

"Sun Court Noble." Valendrial spat in quiet anger.

"Bastards," Sebastian concurred. "He's the host. The taller one is the court official Breganthron's son, Thalow, and his royal bodyguard, Reisha."

"He stole my blood," Valendrial said so softly with rage that the Fae folk around him seemed to take notice of his emotional change.

Smiling at his friend as if he were making a bad joke, Sebastian patted Valendrial on the lower back to redirect his attention. "Not now, Val. They'll walk off to oversee the 'product' loading and then leave."

"It's a small window." Valendrial breathed deeply and returned a tight smile.

"You got a better one?" Sebastian gives a smile that half-moons his eyes. Eyes that, at the moment, were not his signature blue but black, the same as Valendrial's. Seb's hair was covered in glamour to resemble black instead of the rich copper brown that accented the light tan richness of his skin. Valendrial rolls his eyes, reigning in his inpatients. The pair made their move as they casually 'bid' on one vampire or another. Slinking into the shadows, Sebastian followed Valendrial's lead as they crept up on the pair behind a vehicle parked just away from the shipping crew and crates full of corrupt human-made vampires.

"Get in."

"We're just gonna jump in the truck?" Sebastian looked at Valendrial like he lost his mind *again*!

Valendrial looked at Sebastian, double-taking Seb's skeptical look. "What? You want to take on all these goons and cause another police fiasco?"

"Are we gonna do anything cool?" Sebastian whined.

"They'll be easier to interrogate if the situation is controlled, Seb. And you jumped across buildings ten stories high; that's a record."

"I guess you're right! You make me feel validated, Val. I love you." Sebastian with his hand to his chest in earnest sincerity.

"Shit! Hurry, get your fucking ass in the truck!" Valendrial shooed away Sebastian just in time to see the pair finishing their business. Swatting again at Sebastian's puckered lips near his face, they both hunch down and feel the weight of the truck shift as the engine rolls over and jerks to gear.

"So, we high-jack this truck to get to the limo?" Sebastian asks, eyes glowing with an ethereal excitement back to their deep blue. "We're finally doing something cool!" The black melted away to a rich brown, slicked back tidily as he loosened the tie around his neck. Valendrial shakes his head, feeling his emotions surge at the thrill of the hunt. Waiting until the pair had hit a relatively quiet stretch of highway, Sebastian gave the clear on the driver seat, and Valendrial nodded and then pounced, shattering the glass in the single cab truck. Grabbing the startled gunman before he could raise his gun, Val put him under in a single punch and threw the human in the back. Sebastian then hit the driver, knocking him out; Sebastian shoved the human to Valendrial, who positioned him between them. Sebastian moved fast to apply pressure to the gas pedal, correcting the vehicle as the truck swerved.

"Thank God we got our licenses last year!" Sebastian laughs while the human's mouth hangs open, and their head lulls between them.

"Wait, you got your license?" Valendrial looked at Seb in shock.

CHAPTER FOURTEEN

Pulling up to the Christodora House, Valendrial and Sebastian look at each other confusedly until it dawns on Valendrial, "There's a gate here."

"Gotta be shitting me." Sebastian whistles low. "Right under our noses."

"Seb, we got to get to them before they get to that portal."

"Don't have to tell me twice; I get Riesha."

"You have problems." Valendrial shakes his head, exiting the car.

"Says the man in love with a magicless hybrid." *Oh, this wolf's got low blows, too.*

Valendrial saunters in front of the truck and onto the curb, slipping the glamour from his form. The high elf of the Sun King's society council stops, as does Riesha, both tensing.

"Who-? Ah, you're the first," The man looks Valendrial up and down, pausing to add, "Abomination." Grinning with condescension, Valendrial is too old to let such pettiness get under his skin. So, he gives the pretty boy a classic smile, which suddenly fades to a flat and emotionless. He stares at the duo with dead, predatory eyes. "Tell me, whose supplied you with the blood and bodies? Who's the source?"

Valendrial and Sebastian could feel the magic rush across their skin as if seeking to bind them to the concrete on which they stood. Still smiling, Valendrial looked over at Sebastian, who stood equal to his friend, sharing a shake of the head. Sebastian looks lethal as he widens his feet, signaling to the guard, who shares his sentiment of preparedness.

"Looks like the pretty boy and pet here don't want to talk." Valendrial feels his body change and rushes with power, swarming the individual before him. Grinning manically, watching the Socialite's face morph into apprehension. Taking a deep breath, they move. Sebastian first, both opponents pulling knives from their waists like assassins, they strike each other in quick succession of clicks, using their magic to increase his speed against the royal guard; her eyes widen in shock, "Werewolves that use magic! Master?" She screeches out in tangent with her rolling dodge to avoid Sebastian's onslaught of attacks. Gaining distance, the woman pulls out another dagger, but before she can get it fully in front of her, Sebastian has his blade moving through the air; at one end of the black-handled sickle blade is a considerable length of thin chain, his Kusarigama. Looking down at the knife in her hand, she glances up with her short blonde hair dancing around her pink eyes.

"She's too cute, Val. I think I'm in love." Sebastian whines. The blade's tip was in Reisha's hand, and the other Kusarigama was swinging in his hand from the length of the chain. The pair stand at a crossroads. Her eyes widened in shock at Seb's words, then narrowed to anger.

"Don't be cruel, Seb." Everyone who knew of the dark politics of the world knew it started from Toiseach's shifted council at the fall of the Moon Court. The royal guards never gave up on their masters, their contracts going soul-binding deep with dark magic. Valendrial and Thalow size up each other's magic presence; Valendrial pulls his blades from his back as Thalow pulls his hands together. Thalow's hands began to glow with a bright, warm light contrasted with the darkness of his personality. Pulling them apart reveals a silver and gold-handled Cussack's sword.

"Neat trick. I gotta remember to pick that up." Valendrial says.

"Oo, Thalow Breganthron has pretty magic!" Seb teased. Reisha is pissed. She rushes with the blade in her hand, abandoning her weapon, and grips the chain as she approaches. Ducking low, she tricks Seb by coming up to his side and around behind him, choking him with a chain, but at the last minute, his hand intercepts the chain, and they fight for a choke out.

Sebastian's pupils narrow as his body bulks out, increasing in size and muscle. He leans forward, picking the woman off her feet and supporting her on his back, "The only dominating you'll be doing, Reisha, is when I'm naked underneath you."

He reared back and lunged forward, throwing her to the ground. He was in her face before she could get up; with a knock to the back of her head, she was out, but not before he noticed the blush across her face. *Ah, I've made a fan.*

Simultaneously, Valendrial unleashes a burst of power against Thalow. The rush of power only appears as a gush of wind, but in truth, it brings down Thalow's body barrier, making his mouth pucker as if tasting a nasty Philippic. Valendrial squares up, ready. Thalow comes in fighting form, and the Cossack sword is raised. He knew Valendrial wasn't getting out of this one without taking a few hits. The curved sword began to do its justice as Thalow began wide sweeping arches with his wrist, distracting and confusing the angle at which the blade would contact. Val deflected the first blow, raising his blade arm and halting Thalow's sword arm. Valendrial strikes the thigh and up to the arm quickly and two more stabs in the chest before Thalow retaliates and strikes with a wrist twist between them, hitting Valendrial across the legs. And then again across the upper arm. *I took a couple of hits, but Thalow got it worse.*

Seeing his clothes and chest bleeding, Thalow growled, looking at him with rage. "Ah, shit Val, I think he's cute when he's mad too!"

Valendrial laughed, not lowering his stance, "You horny or something?"

"I was serious!" Sebastian gives a classic heartbreak smile. "A good fight always puts me in the mood."

"Toxic ass." Valendrial retorts, but a smear of Seb's words also rings with the truth within him. He felt the excitement thrumming through his veins. *We're not normal, so that's our free pass as perverts.* Hearing his thoughts, Sebastian laughed.

"This pathetic display! You're not going to find answers from me, vampire; you may as well give up before you and *your pet* end up at the circus show."

Get him down so he'll spill the beans, Val. Sebastian says over their mental link. Sebastian continues to goad the Sun Court aristocrat when Valendrial notices Sebastian sitting on the girl's butt like a retriever. *Weirdo,* Valendrial sends Seb.

"Enough of this!" Thalow twists his sword down, his chest bleeding heavily, raises his hand, and a wave of fire emerges. Before the flames touch his skin, Valendrial dives low through them as they bellow upward, like a fire dragon's breath dispersing into the atmosphere. Looking at the building, he sees Sebastian tailing Thalow into the structure. Scrambling up to follow them, upon entering the building, he hears an audible "Shit!" from the front parlor. Closing his eyes, Valendrial feels cold defeat and adrenaline leaving him from the fight as Sebastian comes from around the corner facing him.

"Well, we're off to Los Angeles, and I'm putting in another call to the ex." Sebastian claps Valendrial on the back as they move out to the street again. Suddenly, Sebastian looks dramatically crestfallen as his prized capture is missing. "Oh no! Where could she have gone? Oh, why!" Sebastian falls knees first to the ground, howling to the night sky; Valendrial's eyes roll heavenward as he heads toward the limo.

"We don't have all night," Valendrial calls back.

"Cock block!" Sebastian spits viciously at Valendrial as if he personally made her poof away. Sebastian heaves his body up, sighing deeply, dragging his feet as he walks to the driver's seat. He mutters seriously as he ducks behind the steering wheel, starting the vehicle.

Taking the passenger seat, Valendrial says in a tight voice, "Without the binding removed off her soul, she won't feel anything but loss; now Thalow has gone from this realm."

"..." Sebastian is quiet as the pair begin the drive to the nearest airport, pulling out his phone for flight details.

Valendrial pulls and tears the loosened pieces of cloth from his body, as the bloodied rags annoy him as he heals, "We now know the Sun King's court is pulling the council's main strings. And dear Nim Nim's daddy has set his eyes on you."

"Yeah, fan-fucking-tastic." Sebastian grumbles.

CHAPTER FIFTEEN

Returning from the nightclub, I saw a new guy in the lobby. He is tall with tanned skin, a head full of brown curly hair, and sharp blue eyes. He's lean and lethal-looking. I caught him watching me as I came in the door. *Is he one of my father's mercenaries?* The guy is casually sitting on one of the lounge chairs; his black slacks are crumpled, and he has undone the top three buttons of his shirt. I decided to take the stairs. The guy can't guess my floor number, and the front desk won't know my street alias to give him the proper number. Just in case he is tailing me. I can't help but be paranoid.

I hear the clicking sounds of my heels tapping each step up to the sixth floor. The stairwell is empty, with the hotel staff having their personnel elevator service. On the third flight of the steps, I hear a loud *crack* of the bottom floor door closing behind me. My heart races as I quickly look over the balcony to see him staring up at me already. His eyes are narrowed, and he looks pissed. I waste no time throwing off my shoes as I run up the stairs. Turning the corners feels slow as I hear his boots like a pounding drum in my ears, so loud it begins to assimilate my pulse.

He is gaining by what feels like yards; I swing the sixth door entrance door open. Tearing ass on the carpeted floor and running toward my room, I slam the card in the key card reader just as the man enters the stairwell access. I was running full throttle at me. *Jesus*! I can't get the fucking door open in time before his hand slams on the door frame. Simultaneously causing a panic attack and forcing the blood in my body to run cold. My heart is hammering in my ears.

I don't know what to do! Fight! I turn to throw my body into him and run back to the elevator when I hear a familiar voice freeze my actions as my shoulder connects to an immovable wall of my chest. Hands come onto my shoulders, stilling me, "Calm down, honey. Don't make a scene and open the door quickly. You don't have to fight me, Nimarea." *Poe preserve us!*

"Valendrial?" I whisper in shock. I'm stuck in place, staring into his chest. It looks nothing like him! The quiet hall erupts with a group of young people. They're drunk, pushing each other, and laughing. The person, who I think is Valendrial, opens the door. *When did he open it?* Driving me inside by the shoulder, I am pulled from my daze. "What the hell? Valendr-."

"Who was that at the bar? Hm?" Slamming the door hard causes the people outside to shriek and burst into laughter. On the other hand, I failed to see any humor as the man's face started to change in front of my eyes. His brown hair becomes his signature pale blonde, his blue eyes sink to black, and his sun-kissed skin fades to pale. He crosses his arms, waiting, "Nim, who was that? What's going on?" He holds out an arm in a skewed direction.

I didn't realize how much I missed him. His brooding, dark mood has my heart racing, yet I am angry he is here. "I told you not to come." I stepped back, defensive.

"You were being monitored. I had to come!" Sweeping his hand through his hair. He placed the other on his hip. Watching the movement of his hand, I finally caught his torn-up appearance.

Gasping, I couldn't hide my confusion, "Fuck! Is that why you're hurt?" I came forward to inspect his arm. Each pant leg had gashes along the thigh but no signs of injuries. It's clear the pants were torn from places; it was apparent he had been seriously injured recently. He stood there as if he didn't have nociceptors in his brain. He shouldn't even be standing. *He, indeed, was a different species*; my brain tries to accept what my eyes cannot. Then I realized my earlier suspicion flew the minute I thought he was wounded. I felt a blush heating my face. Gently, he took my hand in his and leveled me with that signature serious look to get my full attention, "Lars knew you were here the entire time. He called me while I was in New York and had me ambushed."

The guard from a few nights ago flashes in my mind as he walks away with Delores and looks back at me with that suspicious gaze. "But the man at the bar gave me at least what information he could." Then something else dawns on me, "Why didn't you say anything about my father when you had me on the phone?" I asked.

He looks at the floor, "I honestly didn't know if that would've made you panic. Or I'd cause Lars to do something worse." He grew quiet as his brows drew together in a pained expression, "I didn't know what to do, Nimarea. I'm sorry."

Again, I became aware of my powerlessness. Let alone not being human myself, I felt human. In all accounts, I was as powerless and vulnerable as them. I understood that when I felt fear over the men and women that graced the street corners at night under the defective streetlamps of purple hue. However, the realization settling in me now makes me feel like an ant among giants. Whenever I slept in the rental, thinking I was incognito, or when I exposed my skin to strangers and plastered all that makeup on my face. Not to mention all that money! It was pointless.

Turning around from Valendrial, I tried to walk away, certainty in my rash decision to be here unsettling me, but I felt his fingers wrap around my form, pulling my back to his front. The chill from his skin causes me to shiver. His breath reaches down to tickle my ear as his arms cover my body to embrace me. "Don't retreat into yourself. How were either of us to know just how far Lars' reach truly is?" He nuzzles my neck, and my skin becomes flushed and tingling with hyperawareness. "But, damn, have I missed you."

Hearing the truth in his words squeezed my heart, "I missed you too, Val." Tipping my head to see the look on his face, he certainly saw my flushed expression just before his lips met mine.

Cradling my body against him, he kissed my lips. I felt butterflies as his tongue slipped between my lips and began a tell-tale dance I remembered vividly from my dream and the cabin. I don't think I can let go. *Not this time.* Bent forward, he has one arm on the back of my head, keeping me lip-locked against him, and his other hand begins to skim my collarbone, traveling ever downward across my silken dress to the nipples beneath. My hips jerk back against him in a shock of erotic connection with his hand, causing him to grip my hip to keep me there. He kisses my jaw and throat, leaving small nips as he goes. I hum in heated breaths, the contact between us so close there isn't room for even a straw of grass. He's hard against my backside, and my body shivers in anticipation against him.

"Valendrial," I say with breathless harshness that makes my voice raspy and without full awareness. I'm drunk on this feeling. I feel my face heat up.

"Here under the moon and always, I'm yours, Nimarea."

Turning me in his arms, he looks down at me, gazing over my features with pure affection and lust. Retaking my lips, he lifts me effortlessly, leading us across the hotel's bedroom with the left-over coffee cups and packets of sweetener. The bed hits my back, soft and pliant, as I am for him. The light dances off our faces, highlighting the antithetical beauty between us. I feel his powerful presence bearing above me like a moth for the flame.

"Wait, your legs. We shouldn't do this while you're hurt." I held up my hands against his firm chest.

"I've healed since before we left New York. No worries, Nim." He smirks.

Sitting me up gently from the bed, he plants soft kisses on my neck, sweeping my hair away from my shoulder, his hand gliding so softly it erupts my skin in gooseflesh. My breath shortens, and my sense of arousal spikes as he straddles my legs. Leaning over me, he takes the zipper of my dress down slowly and purposefully. Peeling the garment from my shoulders, he lays me back, continuing to remove it until I am bare before him in naught but underwear. His eyes sink to black; gazing at my body, I feel the blush already staining my face deepen. Valendrial's effect on me is truly captivating. *It's me. I have his attention, just me.*

"That you do, my love." He says with such prideful adoration and conviction as he buries his head to my lips, tasting me as his hands wander along my curves. There is a hand on my hip, then a hand on my breast, kneading it from the outside, relieving the pressure of its weight on my chest. I sigh in slight relief. He smiles against my lips and gives me this small comfort before letting go to touch my nipples, sliding his thumb over the prickled, sensitive bud. I moan in his mouth as his lips parted from mine. Valendrial's gaze never breaks the connection as he licks my breast, and my hands find purchase in his platinum hair. He stops from under to the top just as his other hand kneads the other. A rush of breath fills my lungs as he gets closer. He licks the tip of my nipple, then slips his lips over it, and I almost shatter from breast stimulation alone. I feel my center getting wet as a wave of pleasure heats me from inside my core.

He kisses my belly, and when he gets above my legs, he raises his head at me.

"If at any point you need me to stop, say it, please. I would never want to hurt you. I want this to be loving and arousing for your first time- our first time." He says firmly. Waiting for my response, his glassy eyes have me hypnotized.

"How did you know?" I whisper, wanting to look away, but he smiles, a very male, knowing expression on his lips. He sensually proceeds to spread my legs, bringing my attention back to what exactly he is about to do.

I want to be embarrassed, but he just made an effort to comfort me, so I look forward to the experience and trust him rather than rejecting him out of inner turmoil over self-esteem insecurities. He touches my inner thigh before moving closer. There is always at least one hand in contact with me; I feel it helps me from being startled by what he does next. So that when I felt his tongue running across the length of my vagina, I was anticipating the connection rather than anxious about it. His fingers tease my entrance, and I feel his tongue insert itself into me as he growls against me in a low moan, as if I was the best thing he had ever tasted. Slow and steady, he builds me. It sets my emotions higher as he enjoys my body. I feel the fingers push into me; his other pulls me closer still. I feel how wet I am against his hand in a few pumps. Another digit meets the first and spreads me open in a way I hadn't experienced alone. The orgasm was rising high and fast. I panted for him not to stop as his tongue flicked my clit, and I rolled my hips, undulating as the nerves released their tightening grip across my abdomen. I groan low and loud, riding against his mouth and hand.

He stands beside the bed to remove his clothes after helping me ride my climax. I take in his body like ashen porcelain against a grey dawn. His muscled arms and toned thighs make me feel like drooling, "You shave your body?" Random, yes, but I can't help my curiosity with a whisper as my voice is scratchy.

He chuckles, settling in the bed beside me, his member hard as it touches my thigh. He holds his arm to me just so as the light catches the tiny hairs on his arm. "I admit I rarely wear anything but buttoned shirts, but no. I have no body hair or high body temperature, so I avoid putting out any signatures during a hunt."

He takes my hand, guiding it to his chest. I feel soft hairs under my fingertips. "Oh." I glance up at him; his eyes are burning with desire as I feel his hum of pleasure rumble beneath my fingertips. I was blushing furiously as his body crawled over me, his looming presence intimidating. Spreading my legs and settling in between my thighs, I feel his member hard lying flat against my very wet clit, and I begin to feel another wave of arousal hit me. Rocking my hips, I rub against him, making him choke out a moan in surprise. I am so addicted, and, at this moment, I can't help myself even as he takes hold of my waist; he hears me whimper as he tells me, "Patience, please."

Something appeared from his other hand; it was a condom. "You planned to seduce me, huh?" I tease.

His ears were tinted pink; turning away and hesitating, "Sebastian gave me these before we split at the airport." He murmured in the most adorable way of embarrassment, and I couldn't stop the giggle that slipped past my lips.

I put my hand to his face, looking at him with the most honest feelings I can name. "I'm ready to be with you."

He kisses me then and grabs himself between us, rubbing his tip over my clit and down to my entrance, and I can't help but moan his name, pleading with him to put it in. His breathing is so rough as he pushes in the tip. His other hand is on the top of my head, cradling me. Our bodies are trembling. I grab his shoulders, stilling at the odd intrusion. My skin shivers as his member enters my body. Our temperatures of fire and ice. It seems different, and

I fight not to detach myself from what's happening. "You, okay?" He asks as I feel he is still only halfway in. Nodding my head, I move my hips experimentally, causing Val to hiss. He pushed back against me slightly in a tentative test; then, we began a rhythm. I get engrossed in building the arousal I'm feeling. I didn't realize he had entered me entirely. As we kiss, panting at each other, he grips my breast, causing my heated walls to squeeze around him in retaliation.

Valendrial groans from the sensation, quickening his tempo as he pounds steadily; I do my best to keep up. He leans away from me, moving a hand through his hair, swiping back, only to have it fall back into place. He levels me with the darkest look, licking his lip provocatively and appearing above me so sensually regal. I had tasted myself on his tongue, realizing what the gesture meant. My eyes fluttered close at the specific spot he jerked his hips to meet. My back arching, I mewl out whimpers to his ministrations on my body. He surges deep within me, firing off my nerves with each thrust.

"You're so fucking beautiful, my heart." But before I can overthink the depth of the comment, he gets deeper; there is some pain, but there is a heady mixture of pleasure, too. "Val, I'm gonna-" I say to him in a rush of breath, gripping the tangled sheets beneath me. Both of our moans came out breathless with each snap of his hips against my own. Tongues clash as our breath mingles in heady pants; something in me is building to a fever pitch.

"I'm going to count down from five. Cum with me, Nim." Valendrial says between breaths. I feel his hands gliding all over my body. I say his name in a crying pant, wanting to reach for what's right in front of me, trying to rub and connect with his body. All of my senses of touch are overloaded.

"Five." I cry out as he slides into me and grinds onto my clit, "Four." I could feel the rush of nerves bunching and my body trying to pull him in deeper. I cry out in agonizing pleasure. Ever deeper. "God, Nim, you feel incredible, three, baby." My voice is loud and rising with each number and praise. He is pumping steadily, but at the last inch, he rams me hard, "Two, ready, Nim. One". He reached around and helped me along, rubbing my clit. I come hard. My vision fades out; I clenched around him as hard as possible, not wanting him to pull away. Valendrial's cock pulses with his release, and I feel every pulse. He gently pulls away from me; I want to grunt in protest despite the overwhelming exhaustion that suddenly sinks into me. He checks me over, and I feel my face being kissed lightly. Valendrial rolls off the bed, and I hear water running. Coming back, he wipes me down with a warm rag. I see a little red on the rag. I am beginning to like a heavy, wet rage myself. He comes back to settle beside me, wrapping me up in his arms, and I nestle into him, cuddling deeply. I hear him chuckle, and it makes me smile. He is radiating with a feeling that is catching.

"Thank you for trusting me, Nimarea. Thank you for allowing me to stay by your side."

I looked over to see his eyes moist with tears. Holding his cheek, I said, "No, Valendrial. Thank you." Then sealed that early morning with a tender kiss.

CHAPTER SIXTEEN

"Sebastian is close. We lost sight of Valendrial, and the portal near the harbor was closed upon inspection."

"Then we have to assume Valendrial made it back to Nimarea under glamor. He wouldn't risk leaving her, even if to track Breganthron's brat."

Lars wrapped his knuckles on the desk. "No, they'll be here soon. Let's prepare a party for them; don't go cheap on the champagne." Lars sat reading through a book. He glanced up at his newest beta and smiled.

"Yes, alpha." The assistant left when Lars called him back, "Do your job this time and keep that vampire put for a while. This portal isn't so easily opened, nor is it right around the corner; timing is key. So," He paused, drawing up from his chair, causing his malice to reach across the room, "I suggest covering all the bases this time. It's only your life at stake if you fail." Shrugging his shoulders, Lars settled back into his desk chair upon the click and subtle *thunk* of the closing wooden door. Lars had no reluctance at scrapping all of these miserable pups. His true ambition would soon be realized. Smiling, Lars wound his hand in a circle, encrypting his desk with his beloved's final writings and account of their meeting one another. It would draw Nimarea here, and he'd have her and the vampire boyfriend pushing the final notes onto the measures.

Glancing at the diary of his dead lover once more, he felt at variance. Like a twist in his estranged heart, as if a dagger had been placed just above it, ready to pierce through. There is something strange in the loneliness of one who has loved once and welcomed the dark after they departed from this abusive, crumbling world. We tend to push away what love once meant and build these towers of imprisonment to guard against the feelings of what had made our cheeks blush and our hearts race because that would mean we still breathed and we still cared. Lars would lose the battle he had already sold his soul for. And sometimes, coming back from the edge of madness and hatred was harder than falling further into self-preservation or self-punishment. It's not regret. No matter what, Lars couldn't allow these feelings. Harboring anything now was pointless; he could never see Nimarea as the treasure her mother had left behind. His revenge was all he could allow. But his towers of imprisonment for his emotions broke just an inch. He could remember her shocked expression. Both courts sided together with them to deliver the news a few months before giving birth. The way her hair swayed in the ever-bluing moonlight, her hands clutching the swell of her womb. It was as time froze for the two of them.

"Terminate the pregnancy, -. It's the only way," Lars had pleaded with her. She looked at him in shock, etching her beautiful, broken face into a confused and crestfallen expression. "Love, please. We can always appeal with the council and gain their permission later."

"Permission? Permission, Hathon." Her beautiful, full hips swayed away from him, her hand protecting her belly. Her hair, black as the night, caught the moon's blue, causing glinting rays of silver to flash through her hair. Her enchanting resplendence cast itself around her white-draped gown. Earrings and silver bangles radiated her regal rage and elegance in such respite that he felt the halls tremble under her pressure. Lars knew now to watch his words.

"They will not stop no sooner than can your people bay at the moon when it passes into your lands. No, I will not give up my child. There is still time." She turns to him, her golden-brown eyes shimmering with tears, "My love, please, fight with me. For our child."

Snapping back from his memories, the desk went sailing across the room, and the howl of an angry wolf could be heard across the villa that night.

CHAPTER SEVENTEEN

Waking up to Valendrial putting me in the shower and calling room service was a sway in a different but pleasant direction. Breakfast was quiet as we were both in our thoughts about last night. Me more than him, as a lot of what I felt had deepened. How do I approach him now? Was there a viable change in our relationship to treat him openly with my feelings? I kept my heart quiet for now, focusing on the task ahead. Oblivious to my musings, Valendrial seems glowing and happy; it is a conundrum, to say the least. Gathering himself up from the small table, he says my name quietly. I looked at him confusedly as the seriousness in his tone changed from the humming, happy one from a moment ago.

He begins quietly, "The magic in my body has always been quiet, my existence just that, never moving or changing. All lying inside of me, it seems like the still water of a lakebed. But the moment I laid eyes on you several years ago, before our companies had met formally. I felt movement. A drive in me to meet you, court you, befriend you. As if my very existence had found a will to move because you were in front of me."

I stayed silent, my breath barely moving as I tried to sink the words he shared into my brain.

"I didn't want to blindly follow you like an animal or treat you as if you were some conquests despite the unrelenting calling in my blood. But how could I naturally meet you now that I knew you were there? I pursued you." He stated this with such conviction. I found his honesty endearing as he continued. "The world you knew has changed, and I don't know how to help you. I hate myself for not being more honest and forthcoming. I have no excuses, but who was I to push my feelings onto you when you already had the world you knew crumble beneath your feet?" His voice sank into the quiet of the ambiance, waiting.

"None of this is "normal." You are not human. How could I hold you to the standards of human social behavior? You're right, however." He looked at me then, his tall, lean body stilled to resemble a statue. His hands, however, trembled. I continued, "The world shook beneath my feet, still shaking. Yet, through it all, you did your best to put me first. You were hurt, too. Drugged and kept like an animal in that darkened room just as much as me, you had to survive out in the wild. You were as alone as I was before we met. But I will always be grateful that you kept me alive, saw to my every comfort, and gave me space and protection when I was lost." I reached out gently, grasping his wrist and bringing it to my chin. I grazed his blue veins with my fingertips before lightly touching my lips to his pronounced knuckles.

"Always." He murmured, staring into each other's eyes; a silent vow was made.

That afternoon, we focused on securing Valendrial new clothes and planned to scope the villa that evening. We entered a retailer as incognito as possible, as Valendrial began to pursue the clothing isles, not wanting to waste energy keeping up the glamour concealing his torn clothing. Waiting outside the hall, it's quiet when I hear the door being pulled, and I lift my head in a panic as Valendrial drags me into the dressing rooms and his cubicle. I worried that something had gone wrong, and we were being tailed. "What's wrong," I whisper.

"Nothing, turn around." His voice is deep and business-like but soft-spoken. He had changed clothes. Now equipped with a crisp new button-up, black suit, and no tie, he was dripping with classic sensuality.

Following his instruction, I turned to the mirror and saw us together for the first time. *We look good together.* I muse as my self-esteem attempts to rear her ugly head. Avoiding my figure in the reflection, out of embarrassment, I place my arms at my side as he looks up from buttoning his cuffs; his eyes connect with my own as he moves forward. My heart begins to skip beats, thundering with anticipation. *What are you up to?* He stands close enough to me that I can almost feel him as his hands come up slowly to either side of my body, not touching, just teasing. I cringe slightly at a cold sensation at the bottom of my throat, and my eyes leave Valendrial's heady gaze to peer down at my reflection, and there at the ends of my collarbone is a simple red ruby-like stone. "It is a crystallized state of my blood with a touch of my magic. In case we get separated, I can find you and show others who your protector is." The tear-drop-shaped stone lay lightly on my chest, no bigger than my pinky nail. The ruby color was deep and almost black in the center. It felt more like an unspoken promise.

I turned to thank him, but Val had already moved, and his form bowed over me, placing a wet kiss on the side of my neck, stealing away my ability to speak. My core squeezes in sudden response, releasing a tightened expression on my face as my body is still sore. "Sorry." He says gently at seeing my reflection and begins helping me pick and dress in my clothes.

Taking our things back to the car, Valendrial announced that he needed to feed. It was the first time he had shared something like this with me, and I would be lying if I just brought home the reality of his non-human attributes just beneath his carefree smirk, "Yeah, I imagine it might be easier than having to snuck deer neck in the bush." I laugh, and Valendrial's face is showered with distaste as if he'd eaten something sour. "What?" I asked him innocently.

He shakes his head, muttering something about never

camping again and "Sebastian's ass."

"My blood cells only last so long, so think of it as a special condition of Porphyria. I burn through them the more I use my magic and coming straight from New York; I didn't stop for lunch."

I gasped in an "oh" shape with my mouth, "You really don't breathe!"

Laughing and shaking his head, he wraps his hand around my head, bringing me close as he kisses my brow. "Be back soon, love."

He moves to leave, but I can't help but ask, "Why not just take my blood? That would be safest."

He looked down at me, and I could see his hesitation. "It's time I have to take. I don't want to risk bonding with you before you're sure it's something you want."

"Does that mean you bound with everyone you fed from? Why am I a special case?"

Val leans close to me, his lean, tall body taking up the space between us, causing my breath to catch. His hand caresses the column of my throat, a dark promise with his chilled fingertips. Cupping the back of my head, he pulls me just close enough for our lips to hover a few inches from one another. Our eyes become hooded by desire as his crisp scent, fresh and clean, wafts across my senses. "Do you not feel it?" His eyes lift to the top of my head, down to my lips, and back to my eyes, "It is not only your incredible ability to survive, not just the observant intelligence swimming in your eyes, but that you accepted me and all I am." I shiver, erupting in gooseflesh as his thumb rubs up along my jaw, just touching the corner of my mouth, "If I were to take your blood, then whatever bond you share with my magic might steal your soul to my own, and then not even death could part you from me." Our lips met tenderly, filled with a deep connection, so much that calling it love, or a promise of desire later wouldn't be sufficient. My heart felt full, and my lungs felt like they'd burst from emotions I never expected to experience. However, hours later, he didn't return. It was getting dark, and he wasn't answering his phone. My phone suddenly rings, and I pick up on the first ring without checking the number. "Hello, Val?"

"Hiya, Nim Nim!"

"My expression falls and becomes serious, "Who the hell is this?"

"It's your brother-in-law, Sebastian. I'm in town, but it seems like Vals got into trouble with Larsy-poo, and we need to get him out." He sounds like he's driving. I remember Sebastian being mentioned by Valendria, but I'm more anxious about what he said than anything.

"You mean my father managed to capture him!"

Yeah, they jumped him and used a decoy-." Looking at his phone, he realizes she has already hung up!

"Ah, shit," He swears and pulls an Uno Reverse, taking off in the opposite direction of Val's hotel. *I told you she wouldn't listen!* But by now, Valendrial could no longer communicate with Sebastian due to the magic blocks and inhibitors Larsy-poo-fucked-a-goat- -drugged Val with. Seb would have to do his best to get to the damned Villa before either Nimarea or Valendrial were sent to Elnolshole.

❊ ❊ ❊

Starting the car, I was in familiar streets adjacent to the

Villa. People were flowing into the place by the yards. Dresses and tuxedos were milled outside the doors, and security was tight. I'll have to get in from the side, somehow. Ducking into the fenced brush nearest the edge of the villa rear, I wasn't aware of any cameras but noticed a window open on the second floor. *I could climb that.* As long as it was dark, and the security was more like AI bots in a game. *Am I now in a video game? Climbing walls to sneak into a fancy party to loot the treasure.* However, I wish I had a particular cigar-smoking gentleman and sassy blonde journalist as a wingman.

Ripping off my jacket and tying it around my waist, I waited a few more minutes until darkness descended onto the grounds. Then, darting across the lawn, reaching for the thick classic bordered window edge, and placing a foot onto the outpouring ledge. Hoisting myself up, I was grateful for the styled large brick and stones jutting just between the windows. Placing my hands on the window's ledge above me, I put my foot on the brick to boost my step up and pulled with all I had to get my chest onto the ledge. Looking quietly and quickly into the room, I assessed that I was alone and rolled and clumsily fell into the room. I had no training, and I was bound to get caught. I needed to find where they were keeping Valendrial. I stood and surveyed where I was.

There was a desk flipped and broken to the center of the room, with double oak doors leading out where the muffled music and voices of the partygoers could be heard. Looking again at the desk, I was overcome with a feeling of getting close—something like a pull in my chest. I see an old scrap of paper lying on the ground, bound together by small silver bangles with unfamiliar engravings. The brown leather held, but the scattered bits of paper were etched with elegant ink and penwork. It was old English and. The name on the top paper was Cressida. Gently picking up the papers, I tuck them in my jacket pocket that's still around my waist.

Opening the door to the hallway, I look both ways in a panic; I have no idea where to go. The stairs were built to circle the lower hall. Looking across the chandelier-lit splendor to see the door open from across me, I hurry to a nearby pillar to my right and peek at where the woman is going. I notice she is in a guard uniform, the wrist cuffs covered in blood. *Found him!* Or at least I hoped it was him. My luck feels like it's thinning. Hearing footsteps from the left of me, I rushed low to the other pillar just in time to see the security guard walk into the office I was just in. Wasting no time, in hurrying to the room the woman had emerged from. I had to play this carefully, or it would be internecine for us both. Making my way to the door, I turned the knob to the door. I waited momentarily to hear anything from someone on the other side. Hearing nothing, I tread slowly inside my nerves, and my senses feel on fire. The room is bright with daylight bulbs and bare of furnishings. But the effluvium of blood and Valendrial's scent of autumn perforates the room upon opening the door, causing my heart to stop and a tingling sensation erupting along my skin. My eyes fell to the wooded floor, centering on a pool of blackened blood. Following the pool, my vision swims as it reaches a concrete slab in the center of the room, to which industrial bolts bolt down a chair, and the figure sits wrapped in chains with his dilated fixed upon me like a caged raptor seeking prey. My heart lurches, and panic threaten to set in, but there was no time for that or the rage in the pit of my stomach at the man I called father for his crimes against my savior. I now knew the deepest of hate for the cruelest of men.

Rushing to him quickly, I faltered upon reaching his confinement station. "Why did you come here?" His scent of copper and fresh forest grows more potent in the room as I take in the blood-soaked clothes and healing lacerations to his throat. They bled him. His voice, as he speaks, is deep yet soft. I feel compelled to come closer to give him the answers he wants. His appearance looks bizarre; there is blood still wet upon his cheek, yet no wounds. Valendrial's features are peaked, and dark circles sit under hollowed and anesthetized eyes. Body poised and severely still, he says not a word as he watches me take in his whole person. He is like a starved lion in a cage that will bite at anything to survive, but Valendrial is eerily without the roaring or showing fanged teeth.

"How could I not?" I say quietly, "How badly are you hurt? Can you walk?" I shake my head slightly to try and clear the effects he is causing me to have. He tilts his head in observation, his impossible black eyes gleaming behind a pursed mouth. The smell of blood is making my stomach heavy, but his scent is lulling me into wanting to throw myself before him and submit.

"You need to leave me. Did Sebastian not come? He said he would come." As if annoyed, he states and begins to mutter. Sebastian's name slips out once. He suddenly stops when I touch his shoulder; leaning down, I can't stop but looking into his eyes. The veins in his arms and around his eyes rush black, but the effect is pale and dim.

I am a rabbit among the wolves; I hear him rumble in a low, sultry laugh, "I am no wolf, rabbit. I am not able to control my compulsion. You need to leave, Nim."

Looking at him with a startled look, I shake my head again slowly. "I know I can feel it." This had his eyes back to mine, watching me intently. "I am not leaving you. So, help me free you, or we'll get caught together."

He suddenly grew tense and still, "He needs us both. He intends to sell us both to the Sun King's court."

"I don't know anything about that place or what he wants. Right now, you are my priority, Val. I'll go look for keys." Ringing my hands before leaving for the exit. Before I could turn to leave, however, he stopped me by saying, "The keys are with your father.

The chains are bound by magic, and I cannot break them drugged and weakened like this. You'll have to go and find Sebastian. He'll be looking for you through the blood charm I gave you. Start at the Hotel. He can help you reach the Elnolshole. Don't worry. I will find you there."

I felt my head already shaking in objection. My breath hitched in my breast. "He'll kill you."

He shakes his head once, shushing me, his voice tight with tension, as if he is losing control of something. "No, he needs me, for now. I will find you, Nimarea. Go."

His white, blonde hair was caked with blood and sticking to his forehead in various ways, showing his signs of struggle. His torn shirt and rumpled clothing are a tell-tale sign of his fight. With a certain amount of resolve, I would fight as hard for him as he always does for me. "Take my blood. Will that allow you to go free?"

Silence.

"Damnit, Val, we don't have time for this ."

He shakes his head as if his thinking is muddled or distracted; again, he replies in rejection, "No, he is in league with the Council. They injected me several times, and it stunted my abilities and magic. Your blood won't help me." He paused, looking at me with shame in his eyes. "I meant to protect you, and I can hardly defend myself. I failed you."

"No. My father failed me, not you." I leaned down in front of him, grabbing his face gently in my hands, paying no heed to his blood coating my hands as his eyes searched my face in wonder. He always sees more of me than I ever see in myself. "You've done nothing but stay by my side and help me give me a boat to float in."

It was a reaction to kiss him. Holding his face gently and with the respect and compassion I felt for him. I wanted to give in to this emotion that lay under my breast. "I love you."

I admire and appreciate that you are in my life when all things seem above me. Valendrial, please keep me with you. There is no courage in me to speak these words out loud. I am inexperienced and afraid of what is around me. There is uncertainty in all this chaos, but I want to know Valendrial and be by him. The whole left in me for weeks when he went to New York, the relief of seeing him again, being in his arms for the first time, melting under his touch when all other men had deemed me unworthy, this Vampire would have me.

I kiss him with all my unsaid passion and loyalty. His relaxed lips warmed as I told him my heart's secret message. I tried to pull back, and his mouth followed me; I smiled and opened my eyes to his desired-filled expression. Pulling my shirt down from my collarbone, I gave my offering to him. Blushing at his deepening smolder, I said tentatively, "We don't have much time. I don't know how this works, so." My words drifted off as I felt this was the last piece of me I could give him and a memory I could take; we'd come to an unsaid agreement.

"I would hold you for our first time, Nimarea. Promise me that after this is over, you will leave this place. Find Sebastian and go with him." I nod my head, staring into his serious and erotic features. Even now, my heart races for him, and tears spring. "Sit in my lap."

"Okay." Gingerly astride him, "Bring your body closer, Nim." I press my body closer to him, feeling the coolness of the chains through my clothes and his coolness beneath my thighs, causing my body, heated by anxiety and adrenaline, to shiver. Moving my hair to the opposite shoulder, I expose my neck and feel his body move upon breathing. Breathing me in his chest, he rumbles deep as a growl erupts through his clenched lips and fanged teeth. I think a kiss touches my skin; I jump a little, whimpering as my hands clench on his shoulders and his muscles tense. "Losen your mind to me." Several sharp teeth scrape along my neck and sink into the lower curvature of my throat. A white flash of light hits my eyes as, in reflex, I shut them, but my mind erupts into a numb, desire-hungry phantom of madness. I feel him in my mind over my body, touching, grasping, pleasuring, all while there is the tender sensation of my blood being pulled from my body. I grind myself as close as I can to Valendrial as he strains against the chains, wanting to pull me against him; the chains send shivers through my body as they contact my skin through my clothes. My waist gets close enough to feel his cock straining his pants. I press against it, and we both jerk in the hot lash of need that streaks across our bodies. My hands wrapped around the base of his skull, holding him to me. The rapture coursing my veins is too much, and Val senses it. Pulling back and licking the wound, I feel a sizzle of heat along the draw of his tongue, along with a slight surge of dizziness.

He breathes in heavy pants of air, struggling against the restraints, his razor teeth still red with my blood. His eyes are closed, and his face turns away, and I know he is fighting himself. Looking up at me, his features shift back into his unaltered state. "Take a lick of the blood you have on your hand." He tells me softly. I do so hesitantly and taste something sweet and tangy with a hint of faint iron.

"Now, we are bonded in a small way. I can talk to you like this when you are close. But it will only last a while until we can truly establish a bond with magic. It is all I can give Nimarea, my love."

"I can hear you," I whisper in awe.

Valendrial suddenly smiles grimly, "They're coming. You have to go." Stepping back and off his lap, I hear nothing but know he means it. "Go back the way you came. The way is clear."

I stare at him with hurt open like a sore, my body simply unwilling to budge against how wrong it feels to leave him. When he says suddenly, "I am your soulmate. No matter how far you are from me, no matter what happens, my soul will find yours. I love you, Nimarea."

Blushing, my hand goes to my throat; I still feel him there. "I-" I tell him softly. He smiles gently, his eyes falling to the floor. We both feel the anxiety pulling at our faces as I turn around and take one step at a time to the door. The last step is as hard as the first. There was a soft click of the door behind me, and something in me shifted. A warrior's purpose has awoken in me. Now to start with getting out of here and finding Sebastian's ass.

CHAPTER EIGHTEEN

Sebastian felt a prickle of heat across his neck as he neared the villa complex. *Someone cursed about me; I know it!*

Sebastian swings the car toward the rear of the complex. Valendrial senses Seb nearby, and he reaches out telepathically. Seb responds, *"Here."*

"She comes to you, old friend." Valendrial's telepathic message is more evident than before but still dull and heavy.

"And I will see her safe, I vow unto the blood that binds us. What of you?" His hands gripped his knives tight upon entering the back fence. He smelled a sweet female scent tinged with Valendrial's. Val's mental energy was weak even after feeding. Sebastian suspected something in the darts and would dive deeper upon their escape.

"I'll be kept alive for now until. He wants to trade me alive to the pretty boy." Sebastian feels his blood run cold at the words.

"HEY! YOU!" A guard shouts and comes to him running. Sebastian's anger reaped a new level against the throat of the individual, and as the blood flew, the compound of wolves heard the cry belt from his lungs as the Alpha pulled back his head and howled his challenge. *All eyes on me fuckers!* A challenge was sent down the backs of other guards who heard the call. Their blood was struggling to refuse the order to submit. The pull of magic compulsion behind it brought the younger pups to their knees while the older ones were stuck fast to their patch of earth and floors of the building. The blast of the challenge rents up into the villa, standing the night still with its authority. A howl follows, filled with darkness, accepting the challenge. Sebastian, of course, smiles in anticipation.

Coming from the back of the villa, a wolf the size of a mid-size sedan stalks out to meet Sebastian. The wolf is red and blonde, its maw hanging in laughter and excitement. Sebastian feels the pulse of alpha energy hum over him, "Ha, sorry, big guy." He says, flashing a cheeky grin and throwing his blade upon his shoulder in a taunting stance, "You won't have me bending my neck to anyone." The red wolf shut his jaw quickly and tightly, not appreciating the attempt at banter. The wolf bounded fast and wide, then stuck low to the ground, growling low enough to rumble the earth; Sebastian opened his body, arms ready. The red wolf, a few beats ahead of him, didn't expect his opponents to charge him in human form. The wolf smugly kept charge as the shifter went to his left; he followed, opening his maw wide to swallow his prey whole. Without warning, a tremendous amount of force had his uppercut into his maw, snapping his fangs together. Jarring the red wolf's head, Sebastian followed with another blunt blow to his exposed diaphragm. Landing roughly onto the ground, dirt and grass flew up as the wolf dug his paws into the soil for purchase. Looking up quickly to ascertain the outcome of what happened, he saw a more humanoid transformation of a wolf before him. Long limbs and brown chestnut fur covered a tall standing frame. His gaze swiftly came up to meet the blue eyes attached to the wolf's form, but his eyes were shining, brimming with magic. Sebastian grew amused as the red wolf stared at Sebastian's form and grinned at him, his teeth flashing white and dangerously. "Oh la, your stare is turning me on, frère."

Leaping away from the Lycan, the red wolf centered himself for another attack, driving a paw against the front legs to dance Sebastian back as he snapped toward the throat. Sebastian countered and dove his jaws down in a quick nip to catch the leg of the red wolf, not wanting to expose his nape for an attack. Defensively stepping away, Sebastian swerves away, retrieving his blades from where he had left them, using his magic to wield them without hands, and begins an attack of his own, nicking and slicing with the daggers as the red wolf dances and attempts to get in close again. Still, the job was done as the dagger scored close to the red wolf's throat and made him back away, quickly exposing his most sensitive part. Sebastian took the offer and claimed victory, catching his throat in his jaws and crunching down savagely. When the red wolf went limp with surrender, Sebastian released him and returned to human form. "I let you live to honor our fight as Alpha's. Show your face before me again, and I will not hold back. Nim Nim, love, come down from the wall. We gotta go." He looks up to see a girl clinging to the side of the building in the dark. Dried blood clinging to her shirt and a mass of dark hair flowing in the breeze, her face a mass of shock and fear. He laughed.

CHAPTER NINETEEN

Hurrying down, shouts resounded as the guards realized who was already in the building and getting. Helping her from the wall, Sebastian grabs the girl's hand. He steers them back across the darkened stretch of lawn. "You know how to make an entrance," she asks breathlessly, hearing feet pounding behind us as we approach the street.

"I do like the attention, " he says sarcastically as he rushes me to the car door and puts me in the passenger seat.

This guy! As I watched the werewolf take the driver's seat and drive the pedal to the floor, He brought me to a black, unassuming car. As he sits me in the passenger seat, a smaller wolf jumps onto Sebastian's shoulder; his face scrunched into a grimace. He uses the opposite arm to grab the nape of the wolf's neck and fling him away.

I reflexively climb into the driver's seat, yelling for the keys. I tell him, "Get in, hurry!" Tossing me the keys, I turn the engine over; just as I punch the gas pedal, I look in the rearview mirror to see a Sebastian-sized wolf standing in the road; contrasting with the streetlamp coruscating glow are two large yellow eyes that seem too familiar to me. Smaller and medium-sized wolves of various colors surround it. "We just missed that shitstorm," I say to myself.

I hear a hiss beside me and glance down to see blood pooling into Sebastian's lap. "Shit, okay, what do you need me to do?" Barely controlling my nerves as the wheel is in my grip, white knuckles tight. *Don't speed too much, but get the hell out of dodge.*

"I'm good. Just keep going east. We'll get as far as possible between us, then hit a nearby airport."
"But you're bleeding out! I can't fly a corpse to New Orleans!"

He laughs, "Voodoo, capital of the US. Do you think that's the weirdest they've seen?"

"Are you ever serious?" I ask, my voice light with the stress of highlighting it out of there. He stares at the road and flashes a toothy white smile. He has an otherworldly charm with his rich brown hair and sharp azure eyes. He has an aura like Valendrial's. It's as if he stands out but blends in all at once. Unassumingly attractive.

Ugh, but this guy's a character! He scoffs in pain, "You do sound like Val. A match made in Fae!" He may be laughing; however, he seems a bit melancholic. It gets silent, and my mind grows numb. I want to fix the whole that is crashing in my heart from leaving Valendrial behind.

Driving through traffic wandering eastbound with headlights trailing endlessly, a sonder effect takes over, watching the steady stream of cars ahead and passing back from which we came. Nostalgia hit when I was oblivious to this side of the world's underbelly, just another line in the passersby. I'm overwhelmed, and a hole is left by leaving Valendrial behind as he feels solid, as if he could somehow put my world back together, making this all disappear.

"Hey," Sebastian's voice is lowered into a measure of calm and soft approach, "I'm sorry. If there were any way I could've gotten him out," He pauses, shifting in his seat; he had made a tourniquet for his arm. He now looked ashen from blood loss, but the bleeding seemed to have stopped. We both have our sense of guilt, but he reaches his right over the glove compartment and grabs something. Before I knew how to react, he outstretched his hand and wiped a tear from my right cheek. I glance down quickly to retrieve the offered tissue and wipe the remaining tears I had been quietly shedding.

"Thank you," I reply without knowing much else to say. I could see his head dip down at my words as he muttered, 'No worries.'

"This has been an adventure for the Sunday newspaper," I say after wiping my face.
He lightly laughs again, nodding his head in agreement.

His puppy dog look makes me want to try to cheer him up. "Look, you've nothing to be sorry for. I am part of the reason he's caught up in this. My head is spinning from seeing people morph into wolves and fight with floating swords. Me, who a few days ago thought she was human. I have no powers. We both feel pretty helpless, but we must believe he'll be okay." *We have to believe in Valendrial.* My heart squeezes painfully again, fighting against my words, but I must believe. I gave my word.

"Sounds like I've got a new member for my fan club. I'll let you know you can sign up for weekly blogs and fan shares through the author's website, but don't be upset to see how many people love me more." He jokes good-naturedly.

"What?" I bark a laugh. *Is he crazy?*

"Only for special occasions." Another toothy grin can be seen in the reflection of his window. *Toxic ass*, I think to myself. Well, at least his mood improved.

"So, you're telepathic like Val?" I asked in shock as he read my mind.

He looks at me mischievously, "No, your lover boy is capable of that, but only through his blood bonding." He taps his finger to his temple.

"But you just did it to me! How?" I grew frustrated that my thoughts weren't my own.

I'm gonna tell her, Val. Think she'll hit me?

Yes, she's gonna hit you. Valendrial weakly mumbles.
Okay, fun!

"It's because your face is too easy to read; you're projecting all your moves, baby." THWACK!

Ouch! It was the 'baby,' wasn't it?

Yeah, sure, Seb. It was the 'baby'. Sebastian could imagine Valendrial's head shaking. He may not have his brother in safe arms, but he felt his family had become pleasantly fuller by the plus one.

Rubbing his sore arm, Sebastian apologized.

"Well, I'm about to lose connection to him. Would you like to pass anything along?"

"You can reach this far out? Is he okay? Should we stay in town?"

"One thing at a time, first you got anything you wanna pass him?

I thought momentarily, then quietly answered, "I love you." I muttered with a blush coloring my cheeks.
Got that?

Silence.

Sebastian felt his blood brother's contentment through the link. Sebastian smiles as he feels the hum of Valendrial's mind as it fades away.

"What's our move once we get to Louisiana?" I ask, loosening my grip on the wheel and checking the rearview mirror for any followers. For now, all is quiet.

"Your daddy is a tough nut to crack, and I don't have much practice with those. But we're not getting Valendrial back, not in this realm anyway. We need more information, with all honesty. If we can find out what House Lars is handing him off, Maybe we can figure out something. But right now, we're outnumbered in both territories."

"Do you have someone inside who can get us that information?" I ask hopefully.

He was quiet for a time, the cheeky mask gone from his face, "An aristocratic slaver we just fought in New York was holding an auction of zombified vampires, Breganthron, part of the Sun King's court, and his old man is on the council."

"Slavers? Are you serious? But Valendrial said my father is trying to trade us to the Council! How does the Sun Court fit in all this?" Valendrial never really got to tell me what had happened in New York or anything about his blood being stolen. I shivered at the thought of what kind of experiments were being made from his power.

"They dosed him with some pathogen that blocks the absorption of iron and nutrients Valendrial gets from blood. It's like it stunts the mixture of magic and blood, a particular thing that only Valendrial's body does. I don't know what Lars is standing to get out of the trade or what the Sun King gets out of this. That's the least of our worries, though; the Council will kill Valendrial eventually, but what he goes through before that." Sebastian's voice is somber, full of contempt, and bridled with such harsh emotions, like a giant storm in the bulky guy, building a tremendous crescendo. "As for Toiseach, while slaving is illegal. The Sun King can't attend court to stop it, and his influence has fallen," He pauses, scrunching the side of his face as if tasting something bitter; he goes on to explain that the Sun King was magically restricted by the Sun of Toiseach as the Moon Court's successor and Queen were put to death. The other's powers lie dormant when the power is no longer divided. This string of events is putting the entire nation under martial law or restrictive government. The Council comprises the former ruling houses of each court that the people select to govern and mediate between the two places for smaller, lesser moves of bills and decrees. Since the loss of the Moon ruler, they have been corrupted in their purpose and unbalanced by the remaining powers of the Sun court. "It's a ticking time bomb and stale mate all at once."

"If that's all correct and this Breganthron person is our best lead, shouldn't we tail them? The politics seemed too simple and were bound to have fallen into chaos. But, knowing that Valendrial's blood was tied to all of this gave me a bad sense of foreboding I didn't want to swallow.

"It's our best way forward at this point. This is the most information we've gained on this problem since it arrived with Valendrial from Toiseach. It's a bit too convenient." Sebastian pulls at his chin.

"Won't they recognize us? And just a reminder, I have no magic." *I am a third wheel, remember!?*

"Well, they won't care about the magic; not all share the affinity, so we'll slap some ears on you. Change your smell." He thinks momentarily as his face lights up with an idea," OH! How good are you at cleaning?" He pulls at his chin, looking at me strangely.

"Um." *There's got to be another way.*

CHAPTER TWENTY

"Oh, is that regret I smell, Lars? That's a good fit for you." Valendrial spat out at his new visitor.

Nathanial Hathon Lars stood at the epicenter of the room, gracefully dressed in a black and white suit that hugged his broad shoulders loosely. He shrugged it off, his face tilted up high at an angle as he flashed his noticeably sharp canines with a wolfish grin. "I regret not interrupting your meal, nothing more." The man throws his coat to the ground and puts a hand through his silver- and black-stretched hair, the only sign of the Alpha in front of Valendrial, possibly one of the oldest Alphas alive.

"I would thank you, but I am sure you have reasons for being so benevolently generous." Valendrial wouldn't put anything past Lars, as he now considered the man several plays ahead of the game.

"And I'd love to ab-lib playful banter with you, Valendrial, but I'm rather busy cleaning up my lawn from that rabid mutt." Yanking Valendrial's hair back harder. Lars' last words come out harsh and growled. Exposing his neck, Lars stands over Val, his canines elongating with the need to tear out the Vampire's throat. Passing his other hand to Valendrial's throat, he plunges a needle into his skin. Feeling a warm liquid sensation at yet another concoction of meds floods his already muddled mind. "I just came to give you a gift and to tell you that even if that little bitch runs to Louisiana," Lars pronounces the state's every syllable with staccato punctuation, "It's already too late; she's as good as caught." Valendrial's expression grows from rage to widening panic at the sudden sensation of displacement. *Where was he again? Why was he here?* Valendrial tries to pull his memory. He attempts to remember his thoughts and why he felt so panicked. He sees a face in his memory, a woman with raven hair and black eyes. *Why is she important?* "Keep me with you, Val." Soft lips pressed against his own. The memory is gone, and Valendrial screams in the ensuing panic. Laughing manically, Lars watches as the Vampire slowly and surely forgets everything.

CHAPTER TWENTY- ONE

Our destination was further than expected. Though the stunning views were nothing short of spectacular, after relinquishing the driver's seat in a quick stop at a din and drive, staring out the window at the blur of passing bush and tree became redundant to the melancholy I still carried in my heart. Hands in my pocket, I felt the weight of the journal I had snagged from my father's office. Sighing heavily for a brace of concentration, I gingerly opened the worn leather cover. The letters roughly scrawled upon the pages of mulched parchment still stood starkly black against the timed, worn pages. Old English is not as simple as Geoffrey Chaucer, the 14th-century poet of my evening musings, but the Old English of the Germanic influence before the Middle English.

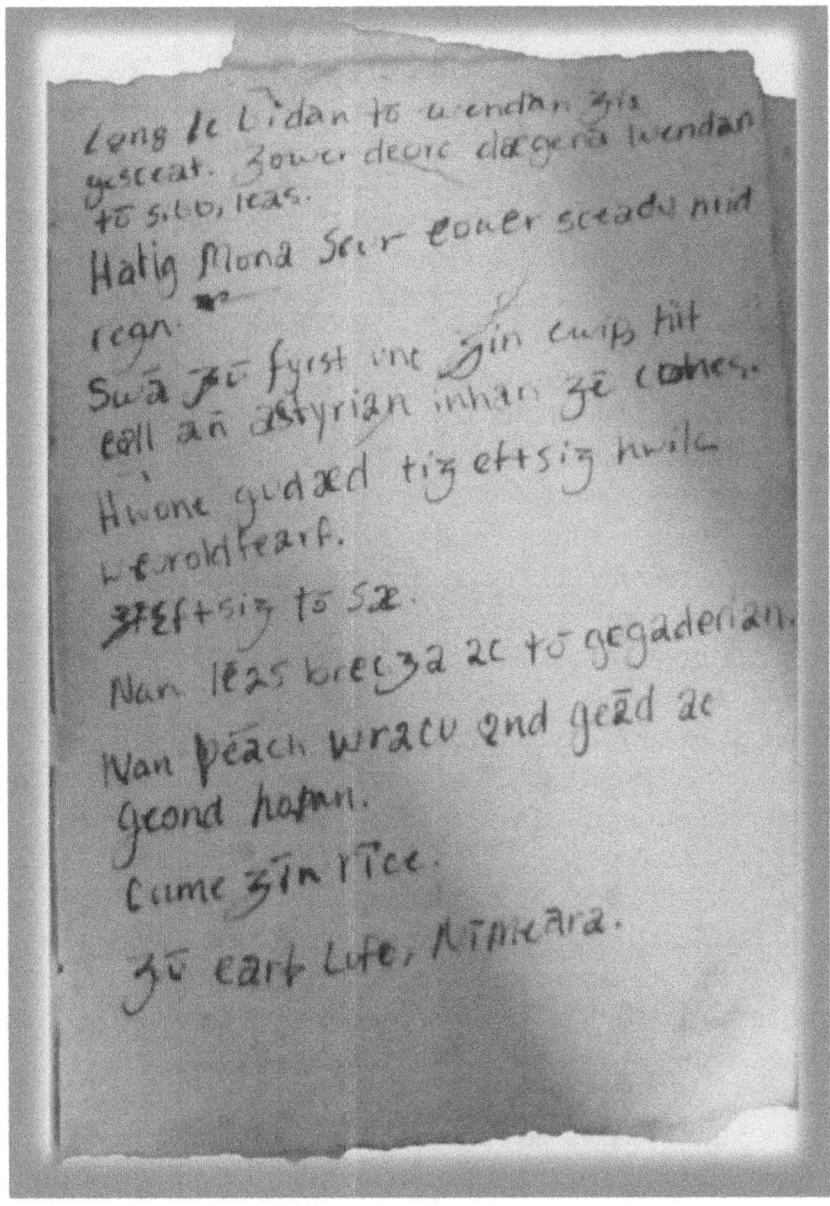

"Geffory Chaucer? I didn't take you for a fan." Sebastian perks up.

"I am, but I found this in my father's office. I don't know, just seemed important." I hear him hum in contemplation.

I began reading. It was a rough, inked smattering of symbols and words. It was a bit more advanced than Geffory's Canterbury. "Valendrial once said that people of Toiseach spoke Old English like this. Would you happen to recognize this?" I asked him, leaning the book into his lower peripheral.

Glancing down at the book, he took it from my grasp, holding it on top of the steering wheel; he began to read while driving. "What about the road!" I asked, looking ahead of us at the sparse traffic.

"Werewolf." That was my reply as he went back to reading out loud. "A wolf appeared today. By night, the Moon named the wolf Hathon. For he is my soulmate. Blessed by the Moon." He pauses, squinting. "There are dates and other information just faded or water-damaged for me to make out." He turns the page, "Ah, here is something. 'To court, called me. For my solitude and reverence under her, I was made-.'" He stopped abruptly.

"What? Does it say what she was called for?" I asked anxiously, sitting on the edge of my seat. This was my mother's diary. What kind of coincidence was this? I couldn't be certain. But one thing was for certain: whether of my father's influence or not, I needed to know what she put in this book.

"She-" His whole body trembles. This is the account of Moon Queen Cressida Lar-." Sebastian let out a laugh. "How did we not see this?" he asked incredulously, but it was to himself more than to me.
"What are you saying, Sebastian? Please."

He looked at me then with shock as if a million things were running in the back of his mind. "This is too much. Your mother was the Queen of the Moon Court, Nimarea."

"What? You've got to be mistaken, Sebastian. Are you sure you're reading that properly?" My mind is numb and blank.

He shakes the book, causing the car to swerve, still as confused as me but just as sure, "Right here! She became Queen of the Moon court! I'm not crazy."

"I didn't say you were, but this is crazy!" I wave at the book, both of us looking at it as if it were sprouting wings. "Well, go on. What else does it say? We need to know, especially now."

Nodding his head, he continues. I hear him mumble before he glances at the road again, "Blessed with life. In her gentle glow, she will be named Nimarea.' There's no date to most of these entries; this diary is old. However, your age and when the Moon court fell add up. Shit, what does all this mean!"

"Just keep going, Sebastian!" My entire body is shaking with emotion. It seems neither of us can scarcely breathe.

"Ah, yeah, sorry." Turning another two pages, worn and ink-bled, he reads, "Do you love me? Hathon, you tear my soul. Would you betray your own flesh? For thou life is now a sacrifice. Moon, grant me release." His voice fades, closing the book. He hands it to me in complete silence. We sit empty but filled with scenes from an unmarked past. A glimpse into their past, one whose memory of that time is only filled with what was written and the other, me, whose only knowledge of my mother was my father's sparse, meticulous mentions of her. A past both Sebastian and I got to see in such an intimate and painful reality of betrayal of the cruelest kind. Opening the journal, I traced the words that only partially revealed themselves to me, trying to feel any remnant of her from the pages beneath my fingertips. Not truly knowing how to feel, I inhale shakingly.

Sebastian murmurs from the car's quiet, "Nim, you, okay?"

No. "Yeah, this is so much." I reach the end of the book. The moonlight illuminates the page through the car window and begins to shine with the script; gasping, I feel Sebastian curse and hit the brakes, turning the car onto the shoulder of the highway.

"What in the hell did you touch, Nim?"

"Fuck, if I know! What does it say? Hurry, it might disappear or something."

"Ah, shit! Okay, um. Long I waited to wendan- ah, turn this destiny. Our dark days turn to sibb- peace devoid of bitter experience. Holy Moon, purify us. I don't know that word. Something about touched: what was done in the past will journey back? Journey back and return to the sea. It's too damned cryptic!"

The page glow receded with the moonlight as it became hidden behind the clouds, but the words remained. "Well, the words didn't fade either way, so I guess we have time to find out." I silverline the weirdness of what happened, noting a tingling along my fingertips as the words first appeared. Looking at Sebastian, he sat back, turned his signal on, and began driving again.

Adjusting his shoulders from the sudden stress, he huffed out a breath, shaking his head, "You never know with this kind of stuff. Just in case, take a pen from the glove box and write that script somewhere."

"Right."

CHAPTER TWENTY-TWO

It had been a few days since we had arrived at the swampy, lush, and dense forest of Morganza, Louisiana. Down in Pointe Coupee Parish, the 136-plus acres of land sat near the Mississippi River, Old River Innis, and Batchelor. As far as Sebastian knows, they were known for good fishing, duck and deer hunting, and endless summer water sports. It's quite a stretch of property, and no one seems to know that Sebastian and Valendrial live deep in the marshy planes next to an ancient forgotten cemetery. With its winding gravel roads of grey pebbles and stones to the mosquito-filled twilight with a cacophony of wildlife, this place held a charm all its own—the perfect spot for magic portals.

We hadn't the time to sit and talk about the diary or the strange, glowing message at the end. All effort had been directed toward the portal, and as quickly as we arrived, Chikondi, Sebastian's ex-lover, met us at the cemetery grounds.

"Why a cemetery? Is this a random occurrence, or is there a significance to this place?" I asked with genuine curiosity. The woods were split with a small pelted-down path to the secluded meadow but strayed too far from this, and it was likely to get murky from the nearby lake beds. Earthy smells of water and fresh air perforated the commentary, brightly lit under the sun. Dainty white and purple flowers were dusted around the base of the graves.

"All places of magic have significance. Most portals are linked to those who created them."

"I see." Glancing around, the area had a certain peace that

set it apart from her imagination. "I just expected something more sinister feeling. Considering the people that put humans here seemed to dislike them so much to cast them out."

"No," Chikondi smiled sadly. Sometimes, we separate ourselves from all we know because of the love we need to let go of to see the growth within. Not every plant can be nurtured in the same soil."

Watching her place down sigils on the back of the graves in a semi-circle in white chalk, she chanted, humming around me. Unlike Sebastian, who was loud and emotional, she was a calm breeze staring out into the ocean coast under a grey clouded day. Her presence was warm, and her voice gentle; I could hear the rustling of her golden bangled wrist and feet as she wrote and weaved her magic in this sacred space.

"There it's done. Let's get back and get Sebastian; we must get you two on the other side soon." She picked up her large tote and placed a single unlit candle in the center. Walking past me, I followed her.

When we got back to the house, the sun was past noon. The smells of food cooking filled the space around the front porch and beyond.

"If nothing else, he's at least good for something," Chikondi muttered, walking into the house.

"I heard that, witch!" Sebastian called from the kitchen. Laughing, I greeted him and found he had several items packed and sectioned along the counter.

"What's all this then?" I asked.

Setting down a bowl of warm food before me, I wrap my hands around the dish to warm them from the autumn chill. "I prepared a small number of things to take along your journey. Clothes, currency, and this."

He slides the small pocket notebook across the counter next to my hands. Flipping through the pages, I realize it is filled with etiquette and court rules. "Now, not everything is like the old days. Many of the laws are the same as here. However, not all are enforced like here, either. Again, magic duels solve the most severe arguments or money, especially with the courts being out of submission."

"You said you'd be with me, Sebastian. What are you planning?" I ask warily.

He holds his hands out in surrender. "You're not getting rid of me that easily, Nim Nim. This is just a contingency plan in case we get separated. Better safe than-"

"Yeah, I think she gets it. We need to go." Chikondi enters the room and hurriedly places things on the counter in the bag.

"Wolves," Sebastian growls and runs off to his room.

"Wolves? They found us already?" I stood and began helping Chikondi.

"More like they decided they've given us long enough." She states.

"Alright, ready." Sebastian comes out in black sleeveless body armor and hakama, wielding deadly-looking blades attached to chains that dance around his hands. Chikondi nods and sweeps past him, only to return with a heavy leather-bound book with a purple amethyst in the center and a pair of silver-barreled pistols with black onyx handles on holsters at her hips. Her black bellowing skirt flowed with her fast movements, each gripping my elbows and guiding me outside.

Feeling the panic set in as we rushed to the cemetery, I saw a flash of movement in the tree line. I whimpered lightly as I felt the hairs on the back of my neck stand up. That familiar feeling of being hunted has now etched itself into my bones.

By the time we reached the cemetery, Sebastian had touched the circle with a glowing hand, and the stones marked earlier lit up with a sharpened yellow glow, circling the area and reaching up around us in seal-like protection.

"Can they get past this?" I glance at Seb. I hurried to Chikondi's side to help her hold the book as she lit the candle she had left before.

"Not on the first try, I hope." He says with a shaken laugh. "Damn, there sure are a lot of them. Hurry, Chikondi."

"I'm trying. Stop being weak."

"Ha!" Sebastian laughs when suddenly knocked off his feet by an unseeable force, shocking Chikondi and me to whip around and find the source. When I see a woman on the other side of the glowing yellow shield, she's wearing golden and black robes and begins chanting something when the pale translucent shield begins to fade.

"Or they have a Sun mage come whisper at it!" Sebastian wheezes, getting up off the ground and huffing. Before I can say anything, he rolls his shoulders, takes a stance, leaps out of the circle's protections, and attacks the woman. Wolves descend to him in an instance, "Don't worry about him, Nimarea. Go!"

I feel a rush of air hit my back, and a swish of green, bluish light streaks behind me in the evening dusk. I turn to see a blur of colors and fractals of light. "How do I know where to go or who to find?"

"It's in the book Nim Nim. I'll catch up; go!" Sebastian yells as his blade sinks into a wolf, hearing the painful howl rent up the night, suddenly, like a bolt of lightning.

"May the Moon and Water guide you." Chikondi kisses my brow and pushes me into the portal, but just before my vision is blurred, there is a torrent of fire and screams. A blast sound roars in my ears as Chikondi is screaming. I hear my voice react to her, calling out after her. Sebastian is roaring in the fading darkness. *No, no, no.*

My sight begins to clear. I am on my back, having been pushed into the portal by Chikondi. I look up at unfamiliar trees and a sky deep with night and stars, unlike anything I've ever seen. Sitting up gingerly, I take in my surroundings.

It was as if Spring was in every corner of this woodland; lush trees, fruit-bearing bushes, and wild ferns coveted the corners and nooks as the moss lay lushly against the roots of giant oak and maple trees. The breeze was sweet with the smells of Paperwhites.

Glancing behind me was a glittering city. Looking as if it were pulled from the pages of a fantasy novel, it held up stone spires and clusters of tiny homes and businesses below. The center of the city was a glow of fire-lit glory as the white of the stone structure of a castle was bricked in rivets of brass and bronze over balusters and lamps, and the windows twinkled with fires within the building. From this far, the scene was something impressive. I can only imagine going closer would make this even more shocking. Let's pretend I am dreaming, eh?

There was a rustling sound in the woods behind me. Turning around quickly, I stood up and retrieved my bag. "Hello?" Did someone follow her through the portal? "Chikondi?" I held the memory of her screams at bay in my mind and clung to hope.

It was always like this, like a chess game trying to expect the unexpected, yet hoping for the opponent to follow into the net provided. My nerves were fraying.

"I am here to escort you to the castle, Princess Nimarea." A rough voice sounded in my ear, that voice. Wait, Princess?

"Valendrial? How?" A deep sigh was followed by the moss-softened footsteps of the individual before me; my heart began to quicken with confusion and a bevy of emotions. Not giving him a chance to speak, I ran to him. Hugging him, I shouted and pulled at him, "Chikondi and Sebastian are hurt. We need to go back, Val. Please, I couldn't help them before the portal closed. I think my father killed them!"

His brows stuck together in a frustrated and confused look. As I looked down, I noticed his clothes were different; he was dressed in a garb similar to the witch. His waist was shrouded in a black sash that harshly accented his narrow waist as he wore white and gold top linen. Armor gold plates graced the tops of his shoulders with matching cuffs around deep, brown leather boots. "What are you-. I don't understand, Valendrial."

"..." He says nothing, his face furled. He looks past me abruptly and salutes. Turning to follow his gaze, I see my father and a young man with elongated ears in more regal garb than Valendrial. Each of them wears an eerily satisfied smile.

"Seems like your witch made good work of the other two." My father crosses his arms. A chill erupts down my spine as my hands grip my bag strap tighter to my chest. *Do I even dare to run? Do I stand a chance?*

"She had better be worth it, Lars." The man says with a frown as he looks at me.

"What did you do to him," I ask shakily.

"Why don't you stay around and find out?" The stranger grins at my father's response. There's a quick sting to the back of my neck, and my hand instinctively reaches to stop it. I feel Valendrial at my back, gripping my wrist, holding my arm across the front of my body. I glance back into his eyes, staring down at me with a face that says he doesn't know me. It feels like forever that we hold each other's gaze when I feel warm fuzziness overcome my senses. Who is this man? I subconsciously feel his hands on my forearms, steadying me against him as I become weightless, getting lost in his puzzled dark eyes, blackened like my mind. Fear grips my veins. What do I need to remember? Wait, that's my soulmate. Ah, I see now. "It's fading." I smiled up at him, saddened by my realization. I take all I can of him, trying to cling to Valendrial like a chilled winter breeze in this spring-filled wood as tears slip down my hairline. I'm ever fighting until my memories fade to black.

To be continued...

www.ingramcontent.com/pod-product-compliance
Lightning Source LLC
Chambersburg PA
CBHW070751120626
46557CB00002B/542

9 7 9 8 2 1 8 3 8 9 4 5 1